Christmas Carol

& THE DEFENDERS OF CLAUS

Christmas Carol

& THE DEFENDERS OF CLAUS

BY ROBERT L. FOUCH

Sky Pony Press
New York

First Edition

This is a work of fiction. Names, characters, places, and incidents are from the author's imagination and used fictitiously.

Sky Pony Press books may be purchased in bulk at special discounts for sales promotion, corporate gifts, fund-raising, or educational purposes. Special editions can also be created to specifications. For details, contact the Special Sales Department, Sky Pony Press, 307 West 36th Street, 11th Floor, New York, NY 10018 or info@skyhorsepublishing.com.

Sky Pony® is a registered trademark of Skyhorse Publishing, Inc.®, a Delaware corporation.

Visit our website at www.skyponypress.com.
Books, authors, and more at www.skyponypressblog.com

www.robertfouch.com

10 9 8 7 6 5 4 3 2 1

Library of Congress Cataloging-in-Publication Data is available on file.

Cover design by Sammy Yuen
Cover illustration copyright © David Miles

Print ISBN: 978-1-5107-2452-5
Ebook ISBN: 978-1-5107-2459-4

Printed in the United States of America

For Tyler

Christmas Carol

& THE DEFENDERS OF CLAUS

CHAPTER 1

The Reindeer

You'd never guess it to look at me—this skinny, freckle-faced, red-haired oddball of a twelve-year-old girl—but I am a Defender of Claus. And I was there to witness the end of Santa.

You think I'm kidding, right? Some kind of sick joke? I wish. But I saw him fall—Santa and his elves and the other Defenders—all at the hands of the evil Masked Man, who turned to attack me next. Maybe you're wondering: Who in his right mind would want to hurt Santa Claus? Well, let's just say that greed exists in this world, and heartlessness, and folks who don't believe in the magic of Christmas. And the Defenders, every one of them a

1

misfit like me, use their powers to protect Santa, to stand up for goodness and for the joy of giving.

But hold on. I'm getting *way* ahead of myself. We need to start from the beginning. Sorry, I know that's a major cliff-hanger. But this is my story, and I need to tell it my way.

They call me Christmas Carol.

Why? Glad you asked. First off, my name's Carol, but I'm guessing you're not a total doofus and figured that out. Second, I may be slightly obsessed with Christmas—OK, OK, *totally* obsessed, which isn't exactly the coolest thing when you've reached my advanced age. But I can't help myself. I wish it could be Christmas all year-round. Santa's a super awesome dude. My favorite colors are red, just like my hair, and green, just like my eyes. And, of course—you know, because I'm not insane—I *love* getting presents. So take a girl named Carol Glover who adores Christmas, stick her in any elementary school, and what do you get? My classmates solved that equation quicker than you can open a present from Santa. *Christmas + Carol = Christmas Carol.* Soooooo clever.

You might think I've got a sweet setup for a gal infatuated with the holiday. My Uncle Christopher, the one who takes care of me, he owns a toy business. Wait, sorry, he owns an *international toy company*, which he named—and you're never going to believe this—the International Toy Company. Genius! Maybe it's not the most exciting name in the world, but then, my uncle's not what you'd call an exciting guy. He sure can sell the heck out of toys, though. We're talking rich with a capital R-I-C-H. But Uncle Christopher's a total Scrooge. He doesn't really like kids, and the only reason he's interested in Christmas at all is because the holiday makes him gobs and gobs of money.

So how did I end up with him? Well, my dad vanished when I was five; no one knows what happened to him. Then Mom died of cancer a year later, and Uncle Christopher, Dad's brother, took me in. But I don't like to talk about that. For now, I need to tell you about the reindeer. You just *knew* there had to be one of those in this story, didn't you? The day I touched the reindeer, that's when the weirdness started, the first clue my life was about to turn to chaos. Forgive me if this sounds all heroic and stuff, but that sweet old reindeer? He led me to my destiny.

It all started a little over a month ago, November 18 to be exact, the day of the annual Hillsboro Holiday Festival. I was decorating my room, like I do every year on festival day, getting into the holiday spirit—well, *more* into the holiday spirit. It was official: Christmas season was upon us.

As I draped tinsel over my door, standing tippy-toe on the edge of my rolling desk chair—yes, I know, not the smartest thing I ever did—I happened to glance down and nearly jumped right out of my festive red-and-white-striped pants. There stood my best friend, Amelia Jimenez, as if she'd been teleported out of nowhere. I yelped, then tottered, then tumbled, pulling down tinsel on my way to the hard, wooden floor. Amelia managed to catch me. Sort of. But we still wound up in a tangle of limbs and tinsel. And the wreath on my door fell off and bopped Amelia on the head.

"Jeez, Carol," Amelia said, rubbing where she'd been bonked and pulling off the tinsel that coiled around her neck like an exotic silver snake. A pinecone from the wreath rolled into the hall as if fleeing the scene. "Are you trying to kill us?"

"You snuck up on me! You're like a ninja."

"*Ay dios mio*, Carol. I just walked in!" she said, exasperated. Everything Amelia says has a Spanish lilt because she immigrated to the United States from the Dominican Republic when she was six, and she throws out Spanish phrases sometimes, especially when she's annoyed with me. Let's just say I hear Spanish A LOT.

"Well, I didn't see you," I said.

"Yeah, that seems to happen all the time," she muttered. I started to argue, but Amelia's attention had already been diverted by the outrageous spectacle that was my room. Her brown eyes went wide. Her jaw dropped. She even gasped.

"Cool, huh?" I said.

"That's one word for it," she answered. "Don't you think it's a bit, um, over the top?"

I looked around at my day's work and shrugged. "Seems fine to me."

"How many Santas do you have?"

"Santa's my guy."

"That's not an answer."

I sighed. "Fifty-eight."

"That's crazy, Carol!"

5

I had ceramic Santas, stuffed Santas, a papier-mâché Santa, a giant plastic Santa nearly as tall as I am, Santa ornaments, Santa mugs, a Santa cookie jar, a Santa music box, and in the center of my dresser, one special Santa, carved from wood and beautifully hand-painted, that I treasured above all else and kept where I could see it at night, the nightlight next to my dresser making it seem to glow.

"You know why," I said softly.

Amelia hung her head slightly and sighed. "Yeah."

"It's all I have left from them."

"I know." Amelia smiled sympathetically. She'd heard the story before, how I wound up with my uncle in Florida, how he came for me in the dead of winter after Mom died when I was six, and all I'd taken from our little house in Syracuse, New York, was a bag of clothes and the carved wooden Santa my parents had given me on the Christmas before Dad vanished. So began my Santa obsession. "Your room does look really pretty, though," Amelia said.

I got up and ran to the window, drawing the curtains against the afternoon sun and throwing us into semidarkness. "Check this out." I flipped the switch on the extension cord, and the room exploded with colorful lights, blinking and sparkling and spinning and pulsating. My decorated tree glimmered. The huge red-and-white aluminum candy canes I'd hung along the wall shone. The Christmas train in the corner blew its whistle and zipped around its tiny track.

Amelia's eyes glowed as brightly as the lights. She smiled again. "Not bad, Carol."

"That's Christmas Carol to you," I said, grinning. "Now let's go. It's festival time!"

My uncle's driver, Gus, was usually the one who took us places: to any school event, out for pizza, or bowling, or a movie, just about everywhere. But this year I'd begged my uncle. I'd promised to study harder in school. I swore I wouldn't pester him about doing anything else for the rest of the year, and possibly into next year. (I was willing to negotiate.) I even insisted I would keep my room neat and clean for a whole month. And finally, Uncle Christopher relented. He would go to the festival with us. A Christmas miracle!

You might be wondering why I was so desperate for him to go, since I've already mentioned he's not the most thrilling man on planet Earth. Well, he is my uncle. He's family. In fact, he's my *only* family. I have no grandparents—Dad's folks died in a car accident before I was born, and Mom was an orphan—and Uncle Christopher is Dad's only sibling. Don't you love doing things with your family around the holidays? Getting all warm and fuzzy and sentimental? That's what I hoped for with my uncle.

I should have known better.

Once we arrived at the festival, Uncle Christopher walked ten feet behind us, shaking his head no every time I tried to coax him into doing anything other than just standing there looking bored. He yawned when we played the ringtoss. (Amelia won a stuffed Santa, which she generously gave to me for my collection. Fifty-nine!) He repeatedly looked at his watch while we rode the Tilt-A-Whirl. (I managed not to barf, barely.) And he rolled his eyes when we tried to get him to feed the petting zoo animals or the noisy red-and-green parrot who had been taught to squawk, "Merry Christmas!"

And as the sun sank into a dusky sky, and the festival came alive with colorful lights that rivaled my bedroom display, I gave up on him. I wanted to see the Santa House, and I didn't want him ruining it. So I snuck away when he was busy staring at his cell phone, Amelia rushing to catch up and looking back worriedly as we left him behind.

The holiday festival didn't focus exclusively on Christmas—there were booths and decorations for Thanksgiving (only five days away), Hanukkah, Kwanzaa, and even Easter, which seemed odd—but Christmas and Santa definitely ruled. And even though it was like eighty degrees, festival organizers managed to create a sparkling winter wonderland. At the Santa House, a huge line of kids waited for a chance to sit on the jolly old fellow's lap, and I soooooo wanted to join them. I would have loved to chat with the Bearded One, ask how the missus was, tell him all about my now fifty-nine Santas, remind him of the whole I've-been-really-good-this-year thing. But Amelia nixed that idea quick as you can say, "Bah humbug."

"If you get spotted on Santa's lap, you'll never, EVER live that down."

"I just want to talk to him."

My best friend glared at me with her big, brown eyes, trying hard to look stern but managing only to look like her usual cute self. Amelia was pretty in a smart-girl, nerdy sort of way. I loved her skin, which was light brown and as smooth as a new bar of soap. She had silky, black hair and a dazzling smile. She complained about being invisible, but I'm sure a bunch of boys had crushes on her. "*Mira, Carol!*" Amelia said. (Uh-oh, Spanish.) "You're twelve! Don't you think you're a little old for Santa?"

I wanted to shout, "You're never too old for Santa!" But I just crossed my arms and pouted. She was right—nothing good would come of me plopping down on Santa's lap—but I *hated* when she was right. So we just stood there, sweating in the stuffed reindeer antler hats my uncle, Mr. Scrooge, reluctantly bought us, and watching kids hop on Santa's lap.

That's when I spotted the reindeer. He lazily munched on grass, the rope from his halter tied to the Santa House. Poor thing. He looked ancient. His gray fur was dirty and ragged, his antlers scarred and droopy, and he panted in the heat. He was fat and round, a fuzzy barrel with antlers. I motioned for Amelia to follow, and we wandered over.

"Be careful, girls." That was the Voice of Reason, as Uncle Christopher likes to refer to himself. He'd torn himself away from his phone long enough to track us down.

"OK, Uncle Chris," I responded, grinning. He *hates* when I call him that. "Carol, dear, I prefer Christopher," he usually says, though this time he just offered up a give-me-strength-Lord sigh and buried his nose back in his phone. My uncle looked about as miserable as the reindeer. He's actually handsome, with red hair like mine, but he has a stern, snooty face that appears to have been chiseled from granite. And, as always, he wore a white collared shirt, gray tie, and black dress pants, which—surprise!—made him sweat buckets. Let me repeat that: he wore a shirt and tie—to a holiday festival! So weird.

We approached the reindeer, which raised his gray head to look at us, the bells on his halter tinkling softly. He had kind eyes, large and round and deep brown, but cloudy with age. I started to reach for the deer, but Amelia piped in, "I don't think we should touch it."

I hesitated. "Why not? He's cute."

"He might be dangerous," Amelia said, keeping her distance.

"This old thing?" I laughed and touched the deer on the snout, right above his black nose.

Bam! There was a sudden flash from my hand, like static electricity, only way stronger, enough to make my body jerk and the hair on the back of my neck stand on end. It was as if the old deer was filled with a huge energy that coursed through my fingers. Even weirder, sparks flew: red and white and green, like Christmasy fireworks.

I was so startled that I yanked my hand away, frightened by the jolt. But the reindeer seemed to have the opposite reaction. I don't know if it's even possible for a reindeer to smile, but I could swear that he did. His droopy antlers shot up, strong and tall. His gray, patchy fur suddenly looked thick, glistening in the Christmas lights. His fat seemed to melt into muscle, his glassy eyes clearing like a cloudy sky turning to blue.

What happened next depended on which witnesses you talked to and how willing you were to believe what their eyes told them. Some folks claimed the reindeer simply jumped—really, really high. But I didn't buy that for one second, even before all the craziness that came later. There was no doubt in my mind that the reindeer defied the laws of gravity and honest-to-goodness flew. I gazed in awe as he soared high over the festival crowd, at least until his rope, attached to the Santa House, yanked him back to Earth.

The deer tumbled to the ground right in front of us. We jumped back as he sprang to his feet, his bells jingling like mad, that goofy smile still on his face. It was as if he'd been pumped full of adrenaline. He tried to run, but he was jerked back hard by the rope. The Santa House rocked, and the Big Guy, who had a girl on his lap, leaped out of his chair in alarm.

Then the deer ran the other direction, scattering festivalgoers as he yanked violently on his rope. A loud crack splintered the air. The Santa House began to sway. Then it buckled. Santa and the screaming child made a jump for it, as if leaping from the deck of the Titanic. Horrified, I watched the house tilt one way, then the other. A falling wall squashed Santa's mailbox. Styrofoam gumdrops on the roof broke loose and rolled away. The house collapsed with an enormous crash. I cringed and shrank into myself, hoping no one had noticed that I'd somehow set the reindeer loose.

But everyone was too focused on the chaos to notice me, and now that the reindeer was free, he bucked and snorted joyfully. Maybe he wanted to share his newfound freedom with his fellow animals, because he barreled right through the pens of the petting zoo, scattering the goats and sheep and rabbits and the Shetland pony, along with the "real-life zebra" festival organizers bragged about on the posters.

The noise was deafening, as if one of those animal-sound toys my uncle's company sells had gone berserk. Brays and squeals and honks filled the air. The parrot squawked its festive phrase as it flew away. "Merry Christmas! *Squawk!* Merry Christmas! *Squawk!*"

Here's where it got really nuts. A tarp that had covered the rabbit enclosure was now draped over the deer's face. He banged off of a trash can, sending it spinning down the festival grounds, spewing garbage. Then he ricocheted off a concession stand like a hairy pinball. Then he slammed headfirst into the pie-judging contest platform, which collapsed, but only on one end. Now it was like a giant sliding board. The table, the pies, and the contest judge rocketed down the slide. The pies hit the ground—*thwap, thwap, thwap, thwap*—making a multi-colored pile of pie gunk, which the judge landed in face-first. He sat up, dazed. A goat walked over and began licking pie filling from the top of his bald head.

By now the tarp had fallen from the deer's eyes, but he was still running hard. I looked at what lay in his path: a roped-off area that held an enormous candy-cane-striped hot-air balloon.

"Oh, no," Amelia and I said, in unison. A few brave souls waited for a ride when the deer came charging past, his antler hooking the rope holding the balloon to the earth. The balloon operator chased the deer and grabbed the rope attached to his antler. The deer, still running at a full gallop, dragged the poor guy, who bounced and slid through the muddy field, tumbling over the grass like a falling water-skier across the surface of a lake. Then I heard a gasp from Amelia. The empty balloon took flight, soaring into the cloudless Florida sky. The deer, as if nothing out of the ordinary had happened, stopped in the field and calmly started munching on grass. The balloon handler, covered in mud, took off after his balloon, but it soared higher and higher.

I still hadn't moved from the spot where I set the chaos in motion. I didn't know whether to run or try to help somebody, wishing I could just disappear. Amelia seemed to be hyperventilating and muttered, *"Ay dios mio! Ay dios mio!"* Maybe you don't know Spanish, but I can tell you that definitely doesn't translate to, "Look at the cute deer and the pretty balloon!"

Suddenly a strong hand latched onto my left arm. My uncle. I wondered if he realized I had sparked the pandemonium. He didn't say anything, but I got my answer by the way he looked around, as if someone might be watching. Mr. Upstanding Businessman didn't want the blame. He pulled me through the crowd, Amelia following quickly behind. I nearly stepped on a rabbit. My uncle had to stop abruptly to avoid the "real-life zebra" that galloped past. Amelia shrieked when the parrot swooped down on her like a feathered dive-bomber, squawking "Merry Christmas! Merry Christmas!"

Within a minute we were outside, the noise from the festival fading. My uncle still hadn't said a word. I looked at him, trying to read his face, terrified of what he might do to me. But his expression was stone, that whole chiseled thing. He opened the limo door, and Amelia and I got in. Gus jumped out and opened the other door. He was a nice man and talked to me more than Uncle Chris did.

"Have fun, girls?"

Amelia and I nodded but didn't dare speak. I took off my antler hat, hair drenched with sweat. When my uncle slid into his seat, he looked at me. I braced for a lecture. But his gaze settled just above mine, locking onto my hair. Just for an instant, his eyes went wide. I glanced at Amelia, who was also staring with her brown eyes as big and round as marbles. I instinctively ran my fingers through my hair but felt nothing. My uncle jerked his head forward, staring intently at Gus as the limo pulled out of the lot.

I looked in a small mirror on the limo door and gasped. Amid the jumble of curls, hanging across my forehead and directly above my green eyes and freckled nose, was a long lock of snow-white hair weaving its way through the bright red. The streak made my head look sort of like the beginnings of a candy cane. Had the shock from the reindeer caused that? I looked at Amelia, who simply shrugged. I sat back and glanced at my uncle, who kept his eyes straight ahead. I desperately wanted him to say something, to explain the craziness that had just happened. But we rode in silence. I sighed and turned to look out the window. I spotted the hot-air balloon floating serenely through the sky, followed closely by a red and green parrot, probably still squawking "Merry Christmas." I watched the balloon and the bird soar into the unknown.

I didn't know it at the time, but with the help of a peculiar visitor about to arrive in Hillsboro, I would soon be doing the same.

CHAPTER 2

A "Decidedly Peculiar" Teacher

Uncle Chris never said a word to me the rest of the weekend, never gave me one of his lectures, never uttered those
two dreaded words—"Carol, dear . . ."—that were always
followed by a scolding. "Carol, dear, I really must insist on
quiet." "Carol, dear, you need to improve your grades if
you want to get into a prestigious college." "Carol, dear,
please try not to destroy holiday festivals in the future."

No, he just shut the door to his study and I didn't see
him again till Sunday breakfast, where we ate in stony
silence. Once I caught him staring at me with a quizzical
look, but he glanced away quickly, drained the rest of his

disgusting kale smoothie, and returned to his study, slamming the door behind him.

I didn't see him again till that evening, when two unexpected visitors rang the doorbell. No one *ever* just stopped by our house—not without an appointment. So I snuck halfway down our spiral marble staircase and listened to the voices echoing out of the living room.

"She did what?" Uncle Christopher asked, sounding exasperated.

"She quit, Mr. Glover." I recognized the voice of Mr. Louderman, who, along with my uncle, sat on the advisory board for Broward Academy, the hoity-toity private school Uncle Chris made me attend.

"Carol's teacher?"

"Yes, Mr. Glover," came another voice: Mrs. Ridgemont, a rich old bird who wore so much makeup she looked like a circus clown, and who had the annoying habit of pinching my cheek and exclaiming, "Oooooh, freckles," as if I didn't already know I had them. "She left me this voice mail," Mrs. Ridgemont said. I heard her fiddling with her phone, muttering to herself about the "infernal contraption" before she finally managed to play the message.

The recorded voice of a panicky Miss Arbogast floated up the stairs. "I'm sorry. I'm so sorry! But I must submit my immediate resignation." Her voice grew louder and louder until she was all but screaming. "I have to help him! I have to help the children!" Then the phone clicked to silence.

"Who is 'him'?" Uncle Christopher asked.

"Don't know," Mr. Louderman said.

"And how is she helping the children by abandoning them?"

"No idea," Mrs. Ridgemont responded.

"And you tried to reach her?"

"Doesn't answer her phone," Mr. Louderman said. "Her house is dark, and her car's gone."

My uncle said nothing until Mrs. Ridgemont spoke up again. "There's more." She hesitated. "We have a replacement already."

"What do you mean?"

"He called me out of the blue offering his services, saying, and I quote, 'Should any emergencies arise.' Those were his exact words."

"As if he knew," Mr. Louderman added.

"His credentials are impeccable," Mrs. Ridgemont said. "He's taught at some of the finest schools. But . . ."

"But what?" my uncle asked.

Mrs. Ridgemont lowered her voice. "He's, uh, decidedly peculiar."

That was the last I heard of the conversation. I'd been leaning in, trying to catch every word, when my foot slipped out from under me on the marble staircase. I tumbled down two steps, grunting with each roll, before I managed to grab the rail. But it was enough to alert my uncle to my presence. "Who's there?" he called, though I'm sure he knew *exactly* who was there. I sprinted up the stairs, down the hallway, and into the colorful, flashing sanctuary that was my room. I flipped off the lights, crawled under the covers, and listened as my uncle's footsteps approached my door. He paused there, as if deciding whether I was worth his energies at that moment, and then turned and walked away. I exhaled, pulled the covers tight around me, glanced at my carved Santa, and fell asleep wondering about the fate of Miss Arbogast and the sudden arrival of the mysterious and "decidedly peculiar" new teacher.

When I walked into class five minutes before the tardy bell, the room was already full. Word had spread quickly about Miss Arbogast's disappearance, and kids had arrived early, curious about the new guy. But the teacher hadn't arrived. Or maybe he had. His desk, one of those giant hunks of gray metal that sits flush with the floor and has a hole for the teacher's legs, had almost nothing on it, except for a single, solitary candy cane. No books, no pencils, no calendars or planners or pencil sharpeners. Just that candy cane, sitting dead center on the desktop.

One of my classmates, Vincent Cato, who usually made a point of sitting near me so he could torture me, strolled into class right before the bell, always the last to arrive. He stopped in front of me and said loudly, "Holy cannoli, Christmas Carol, what happened to your hair?" Vincent was one of the few kids in sixth grade as tall as I was. He had dirty blond hair, icy blue eyes, and a pointy nose. He was handsome in a cruel way, like a movie villain. Vincent noticed the candy cane. "Did you leave the teacher a treat, Christmas Carol?" Everyone laughed, and my face turned bright red. Vincent had a knack for getting under my freckled skin, and my classmates would never defy him—not wanting to be his next target. So it felt like me against the world whenever I was in school. Thank goodness Amelia had my back, or the daily harassment would have been unbearable.

The bell rang, and we turned toward the door. Seconds went by. Then minutes. Still no teacher. The class grew louder, and louder, chaos erupting. In the seat next to me sat Amelia, who still seemed to like me despite the fact that I nearly got her run over by a rampaging reindeer and attacked by a psychotic parrot. Amelia was an outcast like me, most definitely different from everyone else. Broward was full of the kids of the rich and powerful (like my uncle). But Amelia's family was "plain old middle-class," as she put it. She was there on scholarship because she was super smart, way smarter than me, or I, or whatever the grammatically correct way of saying that is, which I wouldn't know but Amelia most certainly would.

"What do you think the new teacher will be like?" I asked her.

Amelia was reading, paying no attention to the bedlam around her. She set down her book (*To Kill a Mockingbird*; Amelia preferred "the classics"), then put her right hand to her temple, concentrating. "Hold on, let me use my psychic powers and I'll tell you."

"Smarty-pants," I said. "Mrs. Ridgemont says he's 'decidedly peculiar,' whatever that means."

"That's cool," Amelia said, grinning. "I like weirdos. That's why I like you."

"Mm-hmm. You're full of them today, aren't you?" I didn't mind Amelia's teasing. We'd been friends from day one, the new kids at Broward when I was eight and she was seven. I'd spent two years in a Hillsboro public school, until my uncle decided I needed "more discipline" and enrolled me in Broward, holding me back a year. I'm not a doofus or anything; I just fell behind after the loss of my parents. That messed me up pretty bad, and it made sense to have me repeat second grade in the much more challenging Broward Academy.

Amelia had been in a different elementary school, where she learned English in less than a year and her IQ tested off the charts. Her teachers got her into Broward.

So on that first day of second grade, we both were sitting quietly in the admissions office, both terrified, neither of us saying a word. Amelia clutched what looked like a letter. I snuck a peek and saw Spanish writing and foreign-looking stamps all over the front. She noticed me looking and pulled the letter closer to her chest, eyeing me suspiciously. "Whatcha got there?" I asked and smiled broadly. I can be quite charming, you know.

Amelia hesitated, looking around as if she thought we might get in trouble for speaking aloud. "A letter that came this morning from my dad," she finally said. "Wishing me luck at my new school."

"Where is he?" I asked, thinking of my own dad, maybe somewhere still out there in the world. I wondered if I'd ever see him again.

"The Dominican Republic," she answered.

"That's where you're from?"

"Yes."

"But you live here now?"

"Yes, with my mom and two brothers."

"Why not your dad?"

"He doesn't have papers," Amelia said, sadly.

"Oh." Neither of us said anything for a long while. I looked at the letter again. "Can I see?"

Amelia looked alarmed. "It's private," she said. "And it's in Spanish."

"Well, I only know English, and my teachers probably would say I don't even know that." Amelia laughed. "I just want to look at it," I said.

She hesitated, but then handed me the letter. I turned it over, studying it. "The stamps are really cool." They were brightly colored and read, "República Dominicana." Amelia nodded. "Why doesn't he just email you?" I asked.

"He does," Amelia said. "But he says he wants to send me something permanent I can hold on to and think of him."

"That's nice," I said. I slid the letter out and glanced up at her. "This OK?"

"I guess," she answered, seeming to hold her breath, as if I might suddenly tear the letter into pieces.

I looked at the Spanish script. No one had ever written me a letter. I fantasized about my father, wherever he might be, writing a long explanation of why he had vanished and promising to return someday soon. At the bottom of Amelia's letter, her father had signed it, "Papi." Then below that I was surprised to see English words. I read them aloud. "I will love you much eternity. Hugs and kisses and butterfly wishes."

I glanced up at Amelia and she looked embarrassed. "He doesn't speak any English," she explained. "I think he found that online or something. It's how he ends every letter he sends me. It's silly." She turned away.

I looked down at the last phrase again. *Hugs and kisses and butterfly wishes.* The words didn't make much sense, but they made me feel warm inside. "It's not silly at all," I said. "It's really nice."

Amelia smiled gratefully. Her eyes misted a little as I handed her back the letter. We were best friends from that moment on.

And four years later, I was still sitting beside her, this time waiting for our new sixth-grade teacher. "I'm sure he'll be good," Amelia said. "*All* the teachers here are good. Not like at my old school." Amelia loved to tell me how lucky we were to have such a tough curriculum. Struggling night after night with a backpack full of home-work, I had a hard time feeling lucky.

Behind me Vincent Cato got out of his chair, bopping me on the head as he strode to the front of the classroom, making the kids around me snicker nastily. "Children, children," he called out in a squeaky, high-pitched, teacher-like voice. "Let's behave now." Amelia and I looked at each other and rolled our eyes. Everyone else laughed. Vincent picked up the candy cane, checked the door for the teacher, and then slowly unwrapped it. Everyone gasped as he took a big bite off the curved end. A pointy stick remained, sharp as a knife, and Vincent thrust it toward me like a sword. I flinched. "Watch out, Christmas Carol!" His mouth was full of candy cane so his words came out garbled. "I'm armdeb and dangerub."

"Stop it, Vincent!" Amelia said.

"Mind your business, nerd," Vincent responded. He laughed and jumped backward, butt first, landing hard on the desk, his feet banging the front like a gong. He chomped happily on the candy cane.

Maybe the crunching was why he didn't hear. Because his back was turned, he couldn't see what the rest of us did. From under the huge, metal desk, from out of the hole where the teacher's legs go, slowly rose a skinny, little man with hair as black as shoe polish, and eyeglasses with lenses so large and thick it looked like he was wearing a couple of magnifying glasses that had been glued together. He held a flashlight and a book: *The Life of Charles Dickens*.

The class froze, falling silent as the teacher stared at us with an odd expression that wasn't quite a smile and wasn't quite a frown. Then came the panic. Kids scrambled back to their seats. Everyone sat up straight. Vincent, who, if you want to know the truth, wasn't the brightest bulb in the chandelier, looked confused, the sharp end of the candy cane hovering near his mouth. He still hadn't thought to look behind him. He glanced at the door. "What?"

Before anyone could answer or try to help him out—most kids wouldn't have bothered; nobody really liked Vincent—the "decidedly peculiar" fellow who was Broward Academy's new sixth-grade teacher, leaned in close to Vincent's left ear and yelled, "Boo!"

Vincent shrieked, "like a five-year-old girl," as most kids put it when they joyously retold the story. He half jumped, half slid off the desk. His feet flew out from under him. He windmilled his arms to keep his balance but fell hard on the floor, bumping the back of his head on the tile. Meanwhile, the candy cane was launched straight up. The sharp end stuck in the ceiling panel like a dart in a bull's-eye. Unfortunately for Vincent, it didn't stay stuck. Had he not been dazed, he might have been able to roll out of the way. But the candy missile fell from the ceiling panel, sharp end first, and caught Vincent square between the eyes. Vincent yelped. The candy cane shattered, and one small bit stuck like a shard of glass between Vincent's eyes. He leaped to his feet, plucked out the piece and threw it, then ran screaming from the classroom.

The class was as silent as a crypt. The new teacher, if he were shocked by what had just happened, didn't show it. A smile played at the corners of his mouth. The kids waited, breathless. I watched him intently, fascinated. I had never seen this sort of behavior in an adult, much less a teacher, much less a *Broward* teacher. Then he smiled broadly, flashing blazing white teeth. "Good morning," he said. "My name is Mr. Winters. Welcome to my class."

As you might imagine, school is not my favorite thing in the world. But when Mr. Winters arrived, I suddenly couldn't wait to get to class. Trying to guess what weird thing he'd do next was a game I happily could not win. He continued to emerge from under his desk in the morning, flashlight and book in hand.

On his third day, I slowly raised my hand. Mr. Winters smiled at me, and I was struck by how bright and white his teeth were—like the color of newly fallen snow. If not for those horrific glasses that made him look like an alien, he might have been handsome. "Yes, dear heart?"

Dear heart? That was a first.

"Um," I started to say.

"Um is not a word, dear heart. Unless you are a Buddhist monk, and then it's "Ohmmmm." He held out his hands, palms up, and closed his eyes, chanting deeply, "Ohmmmmmmmm."

"Um, OK, I mean, uh, I'm sorry." Mr. Winters opened his eyes and looked at me, palms still up. I was flustered now. I glanced at Amelia, who seemed just as flabbergasted. "I-I-I was just wondering why you sit under your desk like that. Isn't it uncomfortable?"

Mr. Winters smiled again. "On the contrary, dear heart. It's quite comfortable. For one thing, it's cooler under there, and I find this state you call home unbearably hot."

"Where are you from?" I asked.

He seemed to tense up. His brow furrowed and he frowned. "North," Mr. Winters said simply. "Where it's much cooler." Then he turned to the chalkboard. Amelia and I exchanged puzzled glances. But the questioning appeared to be over.

The weirdness, however, most certainly was not. Mr. Winters seemed incapable of sitting still. The rare times he did stay seated, he bounced in his chair as if the seat were a frying pan and he was a slice of bacon. Most of the time, though, he wandered around the room, talking, talking, and talking some more, about lessons, life, everything, all while gesturing wildly.

One day while explaining the differences between the executive, legislative, and judicial branches, Mr. Winters stood in the back of the room, pausing in his usual wandering. Suddenly, as if someone had fired a starter gun for a 100-meter dash, he sprinted down the center aisle and leaped, landing squarely in the middle of his still-empty desk. Amelia looked at me and whispered, "What in the world?"

"The executive branch is headed by the president," Mr. Winters said. "His powers are checked by the legislative and judicial branches." He began to pace on the desk. "If we didn't have this system of checks and balances, what might happen?" He turned to the class. "Vincent, my prince, do you know?" That was another thing: each girl was "dear heart" or "m'lady" and each boy "prince" or "m'lord."

Vincent squirmed; the prince, as usual, didn't have a royal clue. "Uh, the government would lose its balance and . . . uh, couldn't write checks." Amelia giggled and Vincent shot her an icy movie villain stare. She, of course, always knew the answer.

Mr. Winters laughed, but in a kind way. "In a manner of speaking, m'lord. But that's not the kind of check I mean." He turned to me. "How about you, dear heart, what do you think might happen?"

I had to tilt back to look up at Mr. Winters. "Well, the president might have too much power, and even if he made horrible decisions and treated people badly, no one could stop him."

"Ding-ding-ding-ding! You win the prize, dear heart!" And Mr. Winters leaped from the top of his desk, his head grazing the ceiling, a joyous smile on his face. I could have sworn he floated. I thought back to the smiling old reindeer and how he seemed to fly. Mr. Winters hit the floor so softly he barely made a sound. He squatted to look at me, eye level. "Remember, m'lady, power corrupts. And absolute power corrupts absolutely. Do you know what that means?" He was so close I leaned back involuntarily. I shook my head. "No one should have too much power in this world," Mr. Winters said. "Even someone who is essentially good." His breath smelled like coffee, but I also caught the distinct aroma of candy cane. "When people get too much power, terrible things happen. Will you remember that, dear heart?" He was pleading now. The playfulness had gone from his voice. I felt a pang of fear, as if his words were a warning. "Will you remember, m'lady?" he repeated.

"Yes, sir," I whispered.

Mr. Winters stared at me so hard I had to look away. Then he smiled and stood back up. "On to the judicial branch." And around the room he went. Only then did I begin to breathe again.

CHAPTER 3

Falling Off a Skyscraper

Life as I knew it changed on my trip to New York City. My uncle was heading to Manhattan a few weeks before Christmas on his annual trip to the National Game and Toy Convention, where he would show off International Toy's newest stuff and see what the competition had to offer. I had been begging him for years to take me.

"Carol, dear, it's not fun time," the Voice of Reason explained when I asked yet again. "This is work. I can't be dragging around an eleven-year-old."

"I'm twelve," I said. (How could he not remember my age?)

"Yes, well, a twelve-year-old either."

"Gus could watch me while you're in meetings. It would be awesome seeing the new toys."

"No, Carol," he said firmly, and that ended the conversation. At least until Mr. Winters intervened. On our very first day of class, he had given us an assignment. "My most loyal subjects," he pronounced grandly. "I want you to partner with a classmate and do a project on a holiday tradition. Christmas, Hanukkah, Thanksgiving, since it's this week—whatever you prefer. Just make it fascinating." I raised my hand in excitement. "Yes, m'lady," Mr. Winters said.

"Would the lighting of the Christmas tree in New York City be OK?"

"Perfect!" Mr. Winters exclaimed. "As long as you're passionate about it."

Vincent laughed. "That shouldn't be a problem for Christmas Carol." My face burned as everyone giggled along with him, but my thoughts were already well beyond our tiny classroom. Every year I watched the lighting of the Rockefeller Center tree on TV, and every year I dreamed of standing under that tree and staring up at its towering beauty, its lights like twinkling stars. Even though

I had never so much as strapped on a pair of ice skates, I imagined gliding around the rink next to the tree as falling snowflakes turned Manhattan into a magical winter kingdom. That would be my project—I knew Amelia would be willing to pair up. And an eyewitness account of it would guarantee an A. I began to formulate a plan.

Gus picked me up after school every day except Fridays, when my uncle required him for another task, something to do with weekly reports that needed to be hand delivered to International Toy executives. I didn't know for sure. All I knew was that on Fridays I had to be in front of the school by 3:15, where my uncle would be waiting—impatient as always. I had been late once, two years back, when I stayed after class for help with fractions. It was only a couple of minutes, but that had been long enough for my uncle to come looking for me. "Carol, dear, you mustn't keep me from work."

So the Friday after Mr. Winters assigned the project, the day after Thanksgiving—yes, Broward made us come back to school the day after the holiday; can you believe that?—Amelia and I hung around after class pretending we needed to "discuss" what we wanted to do. Amelia was in on the plan and smiled as I asked Mr. Winters for advice. He launched into a lecture about filling the project with "gripping details," finding an "angle no one else had even dared to dream of," and "making those viewing the display as delighted about the subject as you are." He was still talking, and gesturing crazily, when my uncle appeared at the classroom door and pointedly cleared his throat.

Mr. Winters practically leaped from his chair, rushing to my uncle and extending his hand. "Such an honor, kind sir. Welcome to my classroom!"

Uncle Christopher hesitantly took Mr. Winters' hand. "Yes, well, thank you. Carol, dear, we must be going." My uncle noticed Amelia. "Hello, Amanda."

I rolled my eyes and said, "It's Amelia, Uncle Chris." He'd met her like a hundred times! But Amelia just waved politely.

My uncle turned toward our teacher. "I really must get to work."

Mr. Winters seemed not to hear or simply ignored him. "Come, come, enter my haven of learning. This dearest of hearts for whom you care is a wonderful girl." He pulled his guest by the arm. My uncle squirmed.

"That's good to hear," he said impatiently, "but I must go. Duty calls."

"Mm-hmm. Mm-hmm. The three of us were discussing the project on holiday traditions I've assigned. The girls are doing one on the Rockefeller Center Christmas Tree."

That's when I made my move. "My uncle's going to New York City next weekend, Mr. Winters." I hoped that was all it would take.

"Wonderful!" he exclaimed. He was nearly shouting. My uncle tried to pull away from the strange man whose hand still gripped his arm. Mr. Winters suddenly gasped and yelled, "Eureka!" so loudly that my uncle flinched and Amelia and I jumped. "You must take Carol so she can see the tree for herself! Perhaps Amelia's mother would even allow her to go." (We had already floated the idea to Mrs. Jimenez. Her only objection had been the money. I don't want to say I lied, but I, um, *hinted* that my *very generous* uncle might be willing to pay for the trip.)

My *very generous* uncle shot me a nasty glare. "It's a business trip, Mr. Winters, and it will spill into the school week. It would not do for the children to miss school."

Mr. Winters waved away the objection as he might an annoying gnat. "Oh, poppycock. Missing a day of school never hurt anyone, especially for a chance to immerse oneself in a new experience. Life is an eminently better educator. I hereby grant you leave to take them, m'lord." Mr. Winters turned to us. "Now, m'ladies, I expect an amazing project. Mr. Glover is making a great sacrifice to take you on his trip."

"We'll do our best, Mr. Winters," I said.

The teacher turned and grasped the hand of my uncle, who seemed shell-shocked. "You don't know how much it pleases me to see all you do for this dearest of hearts." He shook my uncle's hand so emphatically that his whole body quaked. For the first time I could ever remember, my uncle was speechless.

A week later, from seats on International Toy's private plane, Amelia and I watched from high above as Hillsboro faded in the distance. I thought to myself: *Next stop, New York City. Thank you, Mr. Winters.*

Uncle Christopher warned us about the cold. The temperature Saturday was supposed to be in the teens—and we prepared as best we could. Amelia and I wore brand-new lined winter jackets, knit hats with puffy balls on top, and thick woolen mittens that made our hands feel like two loaves of bread in a warm oven. (The winter wear was courtesy of my uncle, who could be a generous guy sometimes, even if he did keep calling Amelia "Amanda.") When we stepped off the plane and the cold air hit me, I expected to be miserable. Instead I felt exhilarated, breathing deeply and filling my lungs with the crisp air as we crossed the tarmac to the airport terminal. I felt like I could sprint down the runway and lift off, soaring over the skyscrapers of Manhattan. This was my first adventure, and it was going to be in the greatest city in the world to see one of my favorite things in the world. I hoped the tree was everything I imagined.

Four hours later Amelia and I sat impatiently in the lobby of the Waldorf Astoria hotel on Park Avenue and 49th Street. We were only a few blocks from Rockefeller Center! A few more blocks from Times Square! And only fifteen blocks from 34th Street, where the "Miracle" happened! *Miracle on 34th Street* was a movie I'd watched a gazillion times, and I'd made Amelia watch it with me on my iPad on the flight to New York. "Again, Carol?" she'd complained, but then was sucked into the story just like me. We watched in rapt silence as Uncle Christopher tapped away on his laptop behind the desk he'd had specially installed on the plane and Gus snored in the fold-down seat across the aisle. I wished I could be the little girl whose mom worked at Macy's. I wished I could be in that courtroom to testify for the man who claimed to be the true Santa.

Christmas movies and shows were an obsession of mine. (I know, I know, a real shocker!) I never miss an airing of *It's a Wonderful Life*. I know I'll be watching *A Charlie Brown Christmas* till I'm ninety. *Rudolph, Frosty, The Grinch,* and even *A Christmas Carol* (no jokes, please!)—I love them all. But *Miracle on 34th Street* held a special place in my heart. Amelia asked me why when we were on the plane.

"I love how the mom's heart melts," I explained. "How she falls for the nice lawyer who defended Kris Kringle, how she believed in Santa at the end and the three of them became a family." Amelia nodded, but said nothing.

I knew it was fantasy, that Santa Claus didn't make families whole, but I dreamed about my father's return, how we would spend Christmases together for the rest of our lives, even someday when I had kids of my own. Or even if that never happened, maybe my uncle's heart would melt just a little. Maybe he'd do more than have his assistant pick out a bunch of gifts for me for Christmas. Maybe he'd be touched by Christmas magic and we'd make hot cocoa together and sing carols and decorate the tree. Maybe it would be just like in the movies and we'd be a real family. Our own little "Miracle."

But real life wasn't the movies, of course, and now we were waiting in the hotel lobby for my uncle, who was "networking" or "merging" or "branding" or something else I didn't pay attention to and sounded incredibly boring. "Carol, dear, I told you this was a business trip," he'd said when I groaned.

"But we want to see the tree," I whined.

"Just wait here and I'll be done soon." He pointed to a man in a tuxedo playing Christmas songs at a grand piano in the beautifully decorated lobby. "Listen to the music."

He led us to seats near the piano, bought us each a soda, and disappeared.

The piano man smiled at us. I was trying to enjoy the music, currently an upbeat version of "Winter Wonderland," but I was so eager to see the city I thought I might explode. "What do you think the tree will be like?" I asked. My legs bounced in my seat, up and down, side to side, squeaking on the leather sofa.

Amelia slapped her hand on my right leg to stop it. "*Ay dios mio*, Carol, chill! I'm sure it'll be beautiful."

I nodded, trying and failing to hold still. "You want to know how tall this year's tree is?"

"Not really."

"Ninety-eight feet," I said. "One of the biggest ever. It's a Norway spruce they brought from upstate New York on a custom trailer."

"Mm-hmm."

"You want to know how many lights they're using?"

"No, but I have a feeling you're going to tell me anyway."

"Eighteen thousand."

"Fascinating," Amelia said.

"We can use all that for our report."

Amelia sighed. "Yes, Carol."

Thirty minutes later, when Amelia and I were lying back on the sofa, struggling not to fall asleep (Amelia actually snored at one point), my uncle at last appeared. I jumped up from my seat, stumbling and almost falling into him. "Can we go now? Can we see the tree?"

"Not yet, Carol." Impatience oozed from his voice. "I have one more thing to take care of."

"Argh!" I exclaimed.

My uncle raised an eyebrow ominously. "I don't want to hear it, Carol. You knew what you were getting into." He turned and hurried through the lobby, Amelia and I following him out of the Waldorf and into a taxi. I sat in the middle, and as we rode through the city, I gave my uncle the silent treatment, which, admittedly, wasn't too effective. He *preferred* silence. I wanted to pout, folding my arms across my chest, but I was soon mesmerized by the sights of the city and forgot all about that.

I'd never seen so many people in my life, scurrying in every direction. I leaned over Amelia, straining against my seat belt to get a better look. We flew down Park Avenue, the driver whipping in and out of traffic, ignoring the angry horns of cars he cut off. He took a right on 42nd Street, rounding a massive structure I recognized immediately. (I had studied every detail of the city before our trip.) "Grand Central station!" A massive wreath with a giant red bow hung above the entrance. A Salvation Army Santa stood in front, ringing his bell. People streamed in and out and I wished I could join them, dying to get a look at the huge interior, which I'd seen in tons of movies. But we kept going down 42nd Street, heading toward Times Square.

On the left I spotted a brightly lit area with a huge Christmas tree towering over it. "Bryant Park!" I yelled, leaning past my uncle.

He sighed. "Carol, dear, must you scream in my ear?"

I ignored him, watching the crowds make their way through the park and its village of Christmas vendors, streaming toward the giant ice rink that I'd read was larger than the one at Rockefeller Center. Even in the cab, I caught a whiff of cinnamon and pumpkin pie and peppermint and freshly baked gingerbread. A short time later, we turned right at 34th Street and I suddenly realized where I was. My heart nearly leaped out of my chest.

"Macy's!" I screamed. The cab driver glanced at me in the rearview mirror.

"Carol!" Uncle Christopher snapped. "For goodness sake, calm down!" He leaned toward the driver, who was probably happy to be rid of me. "Right here is fine."

Amelia and I spilled out onto the sidewalk in front of Macy's. And there they were, right in front of us, the world-famous Macy's holiday window displays. We sprinted over, for once Amelia's excitement matching my own. The displays were amazing: an intricate traditional scene of Santa and his elves in his workshop; a "Nutcracker Suite" with marching toy soldiers; a Jack Frost winter wonderland; a mosaic of letters to Santa; a Hanukkah display; and on and on.

"Come on, girls," my uncle said. We reluctantly turned to follow him, assuming we were heading to some boring office building. Then I realized he was going in. Inside Macy's! Another miracle on 34th Street!

Goodness gracious, I'd never seen so many Christmas decorations in all my life. We followed Uncle Christopher past a massive tree covered in tinsel. Big red Christmas balls dangled from the ceiling. Shoppers swarmed around massive displays of perfume, fancy bags, clothes, electronics, toys, and anything else you could imagine buying someone for Christmas. A series of green wreath-like arches formed a sort of tunnel down an aisle leading to a bank of elevators. My uncle took us to one guarded by a security guy wearing a Santa hat. Uncle Chris showed him an ID, and the guard waved us onto the elevator.

Uncle Chris hit the button for the eighth floor and up we went with a whoosh. The doors opened and my heart skipped a beat. A sign outside the door read SANTA LAND. So cool! An arrow pointed left, but my uncle turned right.

"Can we go to Santa Land, Uncle Christopher?"

He smirked. "Carol, dear, aren't you a little old for that? You are eleven now."

"I'm twelve!" I shouted. Goodness, what was wrong with him? Amelia giggled, then quickly became serious when Uncle Christopher glanced at her as we walked down a long hall.

"All the more reason," he said. "Santa Land is for

little kids." We reached the end of the hall and my uncle stopped in front of a plain wooden door with a sign that read MACY'S TOY DIVISION. He pointed to two chairs. "Wait here. This won't take long."

I sighed, and Amelia and I settled into the chairs to wait. I couldn't believe we were like one hundred yards from Santa Land (in Macy's!) and had to sit outside an office. Only my uncle could make Christmastime at Macy's boring. And I don't know what your definition of "won't take long" is, but I'll bet it isn't the same as my uncle's. We sat there for an hour! I was this close to marching right into that office and demanding to see him, no matter the consequences, when Amelia elbowed me and nodded to the other end of the hall.

Walking toward us, dressed in his Christmas finery, was the Big Guy himself. Santa Claus! His black boots thudded in the quiet of the hall. He tugged at his belt hidden underneath his massive belly. I started to raise my hand to say hi, but as he drew near, he suddenly sneezed. "*Aaaachoooo!*"

"*Salud,*" Amelia said, quietly, in Spanish. Santa looked at her blankly. "Bless you," she added.

"Thank you, young lady," Santa said and turned, thudding down another hall and disappearing.

We sat quietly until I finally whispered, "Do you think that was the real Santa?"

Amelia sighed her distinctive "I think you're a doofus but I'm too nice to say it out loud" sigh. "Of course not, Carol. He didn't know Spanish; doesn't Santa speak every language? And there are a million Santas."

"But this is Macy's," I argued. "If the real one went anywhere, it'd be here."

"Well, assuming there even *is* a real one, wouldn't he be a little busy this time of year?"

"I guess," I replied, moping a bit. Why did Amelia have to be so practical all the time? Why couldn't she believe, like I did? "I think it was him," I muttered, not really believing that but too stubborn to admit it.

Amelia sighed again. We settled back in our chairs. And we waited. Whatever Christmas magic the city had to offer, it would just have to wait, too.

At last! Two hours after the endless business of Uncle Christopher, the sneezing Santa and the doubting Amelia, our taxi dropped us in front of Radio City Music Hall, the marquee trumpeting the CHRISTMAS SPECTACULAR, featuring the Rockettes. I soooooo wanted to see that show, but my uncle motioned for us to follow him and we pushed through the crowd toward Rockefeller Center.

When we rounded the corner and came upon the tree, Amelia and I stopped in our tracks. We stared in awe at the massive spruce, which twinkled with its 18,000 lights and was topped by a glittering star that rose impossibly high above us. We were so dumbstruck we didn't realize my uncle had continued through the crowd until he hurried back and snapped, "Girls!" I looked at him, dazed. "Ladies," he said, straining to take the impatience out of his voice. "You must stay close. It's easy to get lost in this kind of crowd." I took Uncle Christopher's gloved hand in mine, and though he seemed startled, he did not pull away. I grabbed Amelia's hand, too, and my uncle led us through the swirling masses.

I kept my eyes fixed on the tree. I had never seen anything so beautiful. We stopped along the railing to get a better view, though Amelia and I were the only ones to truly look. My uncle appeared bored, as he always seemed to be when I was with him. I gazed up at the tree, inhaling the brisk air and the smell of pine. I hadn't felt so happy in a long, long time. I looked at the rink below and watched the gliding and stumbling skaters. "Can we please skate?" I asked my uncle, who glanced at the rink with annoyance.

"Carol, dear, I have so much work to do."

"Please, oh please, oh please. Just for ten or fifteen minutes. Come skate with us."

My uncle sighed. "You may skate for ten minutes. I will watch. I prefer not to crack open my skull in front of the riffraff." I didn't know what riffraff meant but was pretty sure it wasn't a compliment. I didn't care. All I knew was that, miraculously, he'd said yes.

Five minutes later Amelia and I were on the ice. The crowd had grown even larger (which hadn't seemed possible!), so much so that the man in charge of the rink initially refused us entry. "You'll have to wait till it clears out."

"Please," I begged, knowing my uncle would soon lose patience and insist we leave, regardless of whether we had actually gotten to skate. "It's just us."

"Yeah, we're small," Amelia said.

"Are you good skaters?" the man asked. "Too many beginners out there now."

Amelia and I looked at each other. "Really good," I answered, feeling bad about lying but not *that* bad.

"Excellent," echoed Amelia, the Dominican-born girl who had never even *seen* a skating rink.

The man sighed, opening the gate. "Just you two."

We squealed with delight. "Oh, thank you, thank you, thank you," I said and stepped onto the ice, ready for some Manhattan magic. Boom! Down I went. Face-first. Then, boom! Down Amelia went, falling on top of me. We landed right in the path of an oncoming skater. The man yelled—something it wouldn't be nice to repeat— and leaped over us. He lost his balance when he hit the ice, careening into a shuffling group of four skaters, the five of them ending up in a heap. The man at the gate glared at us. We pulled ourselves up, and I muttered, "Sorry, guess we're a little rusty." We started around the ice, avoiding eye contact with the poor fellow who was untangling himself from the group he'd knocked over like dominoes.

I glanced up at my uncle. He pointed to his watch and held up both hands with fingers open, indicating we had our ten minutes. I turned back to the ice, concentrating on avoiding the skaters zipping by. I was unsteady on my feet but, surprisingly, felt no fear. Hunched over, almost squatting, I forced myself to stand, letting the skates glide. A snowflake landed on the tip of my nose and I looked up. The sky suddenly exploded with beautiful white. I gasped and stuck out my tongue to catch the flakes, which melted pleasingly in my mouth.

I was so focused on the snow that I didn't realize what was happening, how quickly I was moving. "Carol!" Amelia called. I had left her far behind. I looked down in wonder at my own feet. I glided across the ice, my legs churning, picking up speed. I weaved around a mother helping a small child. I leaned into my turn at the end of the rink, maintaining my speed and not the least bit wobbly. How was this possible? I felt exhilarated, so full of energy that once more I felt as if I could fly. I breathed deeply, pulling the cold air into my lungs like fuel into an engine. I zipped past Amelia, who was so shocked that her feet went out from under her and she landed hard on her butt.

I glanced at my uncle to see if he was watching. His mouth hung open and his eyes were wide. Yep, he definitely saw me. I laughed, just as surprised as he and Amelia were. I couldn't possibly explain what was happening, but I wasn't about to ruin it by questioning too much. Once again, I sped past Amelia, who yelled, "How are you doing that?"

"I have no idea!" Before I could even think about what I was doing, I leaped and spun, a full rotation, like the elegant figure skaters in the Olympics. I landed on one skate, gliding backward as if I'd been doing it my entire life. Suddenly a man skated up behind, his eyes locked on me, and followed me close. Startled, I veered left toward the center of the rink. He did, too. I slowed. Then he slowed. I picked up the pace. He did the same. He averted his gaze whenever I glanced back, but I had no doubt he was shadowing my every move. And he was creeping me out.

He looked familiar, though I knew that was impossible. Who would I know in New York City? I glanced back again and was so shocked to find him right behind me that I didn't see the little girl in my path until it was too late. My skate caught hers and down she went, face-first toward the ice. I spun and fell, landing hard on my tailbone. The strange man moved toward me. I pushed myself backward on my butt to get away, but the man slowed and extended his hand.

Only then did I notice. It couldn't possibly be. I must have hit my head and was hallucinating. Everything around me was frozen, and not in the cold way. All the skaters had stopped exactly where they'd been when I fell. The rink was now full of human statues. I saw Amelia at the other end, looking in my direction. But she didn't move either. And that poor girl I'd run into? She was floating. In midair! Her expression was locked in fear and her hands were extended to break her fall. I glanced up at my uncle. I half expected him to yell it was time to go, but he didn't budge. And the silence was astonishing. Moments before, cars honked, children screamed, cameras clicked, Christmas music blared. Now there was nothing.

The man, his hand still extended, finally spoke. "May I help you up, m'lady?"

My jaw dropped. I recognized the voice before I did the face. He wore no glasses. The hair sticking out from under his hat was bright red. "Mr. Winters?"

"Yes, dear heart," he said, pulling me up. "Hurry now. There's much I need to show you."

I hesitated as Mr. Winters skated away. Who was this man, really? Should I just go with him? What in the world was happening?

Mr. Winters turned and saw that I hadn't moved, and he skated slowly back. He stopped and studied me for a moment. "I've frightened you, haven't I, m'lady?"

I nodded.

Mr. Winters appeared slightly hurt by this, but then smiled reassuringly. He looked me in the eyes with that intense stare of his. "I would never in a million years hurt you, Carol. Ever. OK?"

"OK," I said softly.

"Do you trust me?"

I did. I nodded again.

"Thank you, m'lady," he said. "Come." He turned and skated away.

This time I followed and we carefully weaved our way through the human statues. We passed Amelia, who I kept expecting to say something. But she stood as still as a tree on a windless day.

"What happened to them?" I finally asked.

"We just needed a few minutes alone with you," Mr. Winters said.

"What do you mean? Where are we going?"

"To see him."

"Who?"

"All in good time, m'lady." We were near the gate now, where the grumpy man stood scowling at the skaters. "Put on your shoes," Mr. Winters said. "We have to go up." He pointed at the Rockefeller Center building.

"What about Amelia?"

"She's fine, m'lady. When we start back up, it will be as if nothing's happened. And you mustn't tell her."

We slipped on our shoes and then hurried through the motionless crowd. I studied them as we passed: a mom wiping chocolate from her toddler's face; a camera flash permanently lit; a juggler dressed like an elf, two of his batons hanging in the air. Even the snow hung motionless.

"How did you make them freeze?" I asked.

"They're not really frozen. It's time that is stopped. It's how he does what he does."

"Who?"

"So many questions, dear heart. You never ask this many questions in class."

"You never stopped time before."

Mr. Winters laughed. "Be patient, m'lady."

We were now inside Rockefeller Center and made our way to the elevators. "How does the elevator work if time is frozen?" I asked as we stepped in. The elevator whooshed upward. My stomach felt as if it stayed on the first floor. My ears popped.

"Magic, for lack of a better word. If we're not mistaken, you possess that magic in great abundance, m'lady."

"Me? How do you know?"

"The reindeer, Carol." He said this as if it were obvious.

"I just scared him is all," I said weakly. "He jumped."

"You know better than that, dear heart. You know something magical happened that day." He pointed to the lock of white hair that hung near my eyes. Then he removed his own hat. I gasped. In the middle of his blazing red hair, like a reverse Mohawk, was a long, skinny patch of white. "You're like me," he said.

"But why? Who are you? How did you find me?"

The elevator opened and Mr. Winters stepped out.

"Follow me." He walked past a roped-off area and through a door marked FIRE EXIT. I followed him up the stairs, breathing hard as we climbed. Mr. Winters didn't seem winded at all and I struggled to keep up. He disappeared ahead, but his footsteps echoed in the stairwell. "Hurry, m'lady," he called. I heard a door open and bang shut one floor above.

When I reached that level, I paused at a door marked EMERGENCY PERSONNEL ONLY. I pushed it open and was met with a sight that sucked the breath from my lungs: thousands upon thousands of blinking lights shimmered through the snow, like something off a souvenir postcard. I stepped out onto a walkway and the hanging snowflakes tickled my face. I heard a faint voice and saw Mr. Winters walking fearlessly along the ledge. I inched toward him, clinging to the concrete wall. It took a couple of minutes to make it to Mr. Winters, who waited patiently. "Isn't this exhilarating, m'lady?" he asked. I could only nod. That's not how I would have chosen to describe it. "Pee-my-pants terrifying" came to mind.

As we rounded the corner of the building, I made the mistake of peering over the ledge. I could see the

Christmas tree, looking as small as a piece for a model train set. My stomach did a flip-flop. I heard my name. And when I looked up, that's what sent me over the edge. There he sat. Santa Claus. In a massive sleigh. A team of reindeer snorted and pawed in the snowy night. Dizziness took hold. My knees buckled. My hand slipped from the concrete wall. I felt myself falling. Down toward the tree and my uncle and Amelia. Down toward my end.

When I woke up from my fainting spell, Mr. Winters's face peered worriedly into mine. I blinked, trying to orient myself. I sensed we were moving. I was on my back, in Mr. Winters's arms. He was sitting on something, which my back rested against. It was soft but solid. I glanced one direction and saw the shimmering tree far below. I cried out and threw my arms around Mr. Winters's neck. "Don't worry, m'lady. We've got you."

"We?" Then I noticed the antlers. Mr. Winters and I were on a reindeer. We were flying! "How did you catch me in time?"

"I froze you, like the people below, then borrowed one of the Big Guy's team. Happens all the time with the elves. They're always falling off the sleigh."

"Elves?"

"Yes, m'lady. Clumsy rascals."

"Clumsy," I muttered softly. "Elves . . . Santa . . ."

Mr. Winters raised an eyebrow. "Are you all right, dear heart?"

"Am I all right? I'm flying on a reindeer with my sixth-grade teacher. And everyone's frozen. And over there is Santa and his sleigh. No, I'm not all right! I'm freaked out, Mr. Winters! That is your name, isn't it?"

"Yes, m'lady."

"Why am I here? What do you want from me?"

"Everything, Carol." Mr. Winters's face, which never seemed to go without a smile, turned as dark as the night sky. "Santa's in danger, and you may be our last hope."

A chill tickled my spine. "But what can I do?" I asked softly. "I'm just . . . me."

"And what do you mean by that?" Mr. Winters asked. "Just a kid? Just a girl?"

I said nothing.

"Shame on you, m'lady," he said firmly. "Joan of Arc was *just a girl*. Anne Frank was *just a girl*. A girl is a power-ful, powerful thing. Never doubt your worth."

I nodded dumbly. I sure didn't feel powerful. The reindeer circled around behind Santa's sleigh and landed gently on the snowy ledge. Mr. Winters jumped off with me in his arms and set me down softly. I looked at Santa, and he stared back at me with kind eyes.

"Hello, Carol," he said.

"Um, hi, Santa," I answered. I didn't know what to do or what to say.

"We need your assistance," Santa said. "Will you help us?" His voice was as soft as a pillow. Yet I could hear every word clearly, as if he talked directly into my ear.

"Why me?"

"You're special, Carol," Santa said. Special? Me? No way. "Haven't you always known deep down inside that there is something wonderful about you? That your extraordinary love for Christmas means something?" Something stirred within me, a sense of recognition. I thought of how I felt so out of place at school, how I hated being constantly teased and called "Christmas Carol," but how even with all of that, I took an odd sort of pride in the nickname. "I know it sounds strange, dear," Santa said, "but we believe you have the gift."

My heart swelled, as if Santa's voice itself were magic. "What gift?" I asked.

"The power to be a Defender," Santa pronounced grandly.

I thought my heart might burst. "Defender? Of what?"

"Me, I'm sorry to say. There are those who might do me harm."

"Who would want to hurt Santa?"

"It's been a long time since anyone tried. I can tell you that story some other time. But that's where my protectors come in. They call themselves the Defenders of Claus. A bit dramatic, if you ask me, but it seems to make them happy." Santa winked at Mr. Winters. "The title's been mostly ceremonial for centuries. Their main job is to help me deliver toys. But over the past several years, Defenders have started disappearing, including your father."

"My dad was a Defender?"

"Yes, sweetheart."

"What happened to him?"

"We don't know."

My heart ached to hear Santa say that. "I really miss him."

"I know you do, honey. As do we. But he's not the only one. Defenders simply vanish, and we're trying to figure out why."

"This is a war, Carol," Mr. Winters said quietly, and I shuddered. "If something happens to Santa, Christmas as we know it will end. We need reinforcements to stop that from happening."

"Like me?" I asked meekly.

"I hate it, dear," Santa said. "You're much too young. Defenders usually don't begin training until they're fifteen or so. But what you did to that reindeer revealed to us you have great power."

"I couldn't have done that at twelve, dear heart," Mr. Winters said.

"But all I did was touch him," I argued.

"You fueled him," Mr. Winters explained. "You filled him with Christmas magic and joy, both of which you possess in great abundance. Had that been a young, healthy deer, he might have flown away."

"Defenders make reindeer fly?"

"Among other things," Mr. Winters said. "We manipulate the web of time and space. Freeze it, move through it, all kinds of things. But I can explain all that later, m'lady. Now you must make a decision."

"And it's a difficult one, Carol," Santa said gravely. "No one will think less of you if you choose not to join us. You may be in great danger. That's a lot to ask of someone so young. But we need your help. Will you join us?"

I had begun shaking, and not from the cold. Would I really be in danger? Would I vanish like my father? A girl may be a powerful thing, but this girl was scared out of her mind. Yet here was Santa Claus, the man who reigned over the season I loved, the guy I had fifty-nine versions of surrounding me in my room, here he was, asking for my help. How could I possibly say no?

I stood up a little taller, trying to look brave, but terrified at what I was about to do. "Yes," I said quietly. "I will join you."

Santa nodded solemnly. He didn't smile. He reached out and touched my cheek with his fingertips. A warmth flooded through my body, like eating chicken noodle soup when you're shivering from the flu. My fears vanished. I felt as alive as I had on the rink below. I wondered if this was how that sweet, old reindeer felt when I touched him.

Mr. Winters put his hand on my shoulder. "We must go, dear heart."

Santa pulled his hand from my cheek and smiled. It was one of those sad smiles, the kind you see at a funeral where people are remembering something wonderful about the person no longer with them.

"Take good care of her, Winters," Santa said. There was a sternness to his voice, a general addressing one of his troops. "Start her training. When the time is right, we will bring her to the North Pole." My heart thumped at the thought of that. What did he mean? Would I *live* at the North Pole?

"Yes, sir," Mr. Winters answered briskly, and I almost expected him to salute. But he tugged gently on my shoulder. Santa gave me a quick wave, snapped the reins to his reindeer team and yelled, "Haaaa!" Off he flew, into the snowy night.

Before we exited Rockefeller Center, through the glass doors looking out on the street, I caught a glimpse of movement, a passing shadow. Or I thought I did. It looked like the figure of a man, slinking in the night, trying not to be seen. "Impossible, dear heart," Mr. Winters said when I told him. "No one can move." I nodded, not putting up an argument. I no longer trusted what my eyes saw, not after the craziness I'd just witnessed. I was still dazed by what had happened. I had just had a conversation with Santa Claus! We made our way through the human statues on the sidewalk, back toward the ice rink. I glanced at my frozen uncle.

"Why didn't Santa just come to Florida to tell me all this?"

"He wanted me to monitor you, to see if you had the proper amount of Christmas spirit," Mr. Winters said. "The homework assignment was a small test of that." He laughed. "Safe to say you passed. Then when you mentioned your uncle's trip, it seemed like the perfect opportunity. And when I saw what you did on the ice, and how the Christmas spirit filled you . . ." He shook his head in awe. "Come, m'lady."

We hurried to the ice, putting on the skates we left behind. We skated past Amelia, back to where I'd fallen.

Mr. Winters positioned me on my butt, just as I'd been before he'd stopped time. He stepped back, studying his work, and gave a nod of approval. He glanced at the hovering little girl I'd tripped. He lowered her out of midair until she lay on the ice. "This way she'll slide, not fall," he said.

Mr. Winters put on his hat, pulling it low so his red-and-white hair was concealed. "Farewell, m'lady. I shall see you at Broward. We have much to do." He turned quickly and skated off before I could ask what he meant. He waved his hand ever so slightly as he left the rink. The world exploded back to life. The girl slid past me. Skaters whizzed by. The snow fell. Horns and music blared. Amelia struggled to stay on her feet. I glanced up at my uncle, who pointed at his watch and waved me toward him. I looked at my own watch. It had been only five minutes since Amelia and I had taken to the ice. My uncle wasn't keeping his promise. But I wouldn't argue for more time. Little did he know, time was now on my side.

CHAPTER 4

Trained in a Freezer

When time started again and Mr. Winters disappeared into the crowd, Amelia carefully skated over to where I'd fallen. I sat, trying to digest everything that had just happened.

"Are you hurt?" Amelia asked.

"No," I answered. She helped me up.

"How did . . . ?" she started to ask. "I mean, where did you . . . ?"

"I have no idea," I said. "Maybe I skated with my parents when I was little. And it's like our gym teacher says, muscle memory."

"Your muscles must be geniuses."

I laughed. "Come on. My uncle's waving for us to go."

When we got up to where he waited, he was strangely silent. He took us both by the hand and led us quickly through the crowd. As we rounded the corner away from the tree, I turned to give it one final look. Who would have guessed that the beautiful Norway spruce would be the least exciting part of my trip to Rockefeller Center?

You'd think two days of walking around a toy convention with your best friend would be the coolest thing ever. But it got real old real quick. For one thing, we were the only kids there. And second, you couldn't really play with the toys, and most weren't even on sale yet so you couldn't go buy them. And last, compared with flying on a reindeer and meeting Santa himself, the convention was a letdown. My mind was elsewhere—on Mr. Winters and my training, on possibly moving to the North Pole, on whether I was truly cut out to be a Defender—so the convention was ho-hum. But I didn't dare tell my uncle we were bored. I just kept my mouth shut and tried to remember that we were in the greatest city in the world when we should have been sitting in class.

On Monday, the final day of the convention, Amelia and I sat at the International Toy booth, bored beyond words. I was ready to go home. We had nearly finished our project, using pine needles, posters, photos, even buying souvenir props of the tree and Rockefeller Center to illustrate the whole experience. We planned on finishing during the plane ride home, and both of us felt certain Mr. Winters would be impressed with the "passion" in our work.

My uncle was chatting with one of his suppliers when a small red-faced man came charging up to them. Had Gus not stepped in, the guy might very well have bopped Uncle Christopher on the nose. As it was, the man began screaming at my uncle, drawing stares from the dwindling convention crowd.

"What gives you the right?" he yelled. "I built that company from the ground up."

Gus wedged himself between his boss and the screamer. My uncle stared at the tiny man with a blank expression. "It's just business, Milton."

"It's not business," he screamed. "It's my life!"

"You're a wealthy man now. We paid market value."

"I don't care about the money, you jerk," the man cried and lunged at my uncle. But Gus was a huge, burly guy whose muscles bulged through his tight shirts, and he held the man back as easily as he might a child. Two security guards pulled the man away. "I loved that company," he screamed. "You're heartless."

"It's business," Uncle Christopher repeated and turned away as the man's screams faded in the distance. If any of this bothered my uncle, he certainly didn't show it.

Amelia and I watched in silence, looking at each other uncomfortably. I felt sorry for the man but knew better than to say anything. My uncle didn't like to talk about his company with me. "Maybe when you're older," the Voice of Reason would say.

But I thought about the man all day and continued to that evening on the plane ride home, as Amelia and I put the finishing touches on our project and my uncle worked at his desk. He would type for a while on his laptop, then lean back in his chair, picking up something I was surprised to see: a black rock, polished to a shine, with the International Toy logo—a capital "I" inside a circle—carved into it. He usually kept the rock in his office at International Toy, perched atop a tiny pedestal, like some sort of trophy. I picked it up once while I was waiting for him to finish work, and he nearly blew a gasket. "Put that down this instant!" he snapped. I hastily dropped the rock back on the pedestal, too hard, and the glass stand cracked. "Blast it, Carol! Must you destroy everything?" He took a deep breath, trying to regain his composure. He checked the rock for damage.

"What is it?" I asked tentatively.

He looked at me, his face as hard as the stone he held in his hands. "It was a gift. A long time ago." And he would say no more about it. He had a new pedestal by the next day, and I never dared to touch the rock again. So it was surprising to see him holding the black stone on the plane, rubbing its smooth surface as he sat there lost in thought.

Still thinking about the little man at the convention, I gathered my courage. "Uncle Christopher," I said. He looked up from polishing the stone. "Thank you for taking us to New York. We had a great time."

"Yes, thank you, sir," Amelia said. "It was an amazing experience."

My uncle nodded. "You're welcome, girls. I hope you found it educational." He carefully set the stone on the desk and turned back to his laptop.

"We did," I said, trying not to lose my nerve. "Can I ask you one more thing?"

My uncle let out his patented give-me-strength-Lord sigh. "What is it, Carol?"

I glanced at Amelia, who looked nervous. "Why was that man so mad at you today? Why did he say those things?"

My uncle studied me and finally said, "Carol, dear, I really don't like to talk about my business." He picked up the stone once again, rubbing the "I" with his thumb. "But I suppose this can be a lesson in economics. The man owned a small toy company, which International Toy purchased."

"But it sounded like he didn't want to sell," I said.

"He didn't, but his shareholders did, and we forced the issue. They sometimes call it a hostile takeover."

"Hostile?" Amelia said, and I was surprised she spoke up. From the terrified look on her face, she was just as surprised. But Amelia was the most curious kid I knew, the kind teachers love. "What does that mean?"

"It's a financial term," my uncle explained. Despite his reluctance to talk business with us, I got the sense that he enjoyed recounting his triumph. He leaned forward and set the stone on the desk. "My company is in the business of making toys and beating our competitors. And to do that, we have to stay strong. Sometimes that means absorbing smaller companies."

"But doesn't it bother you to see him so upset over losing his company?" I asked.

My uncle showed just a hint of a smile. "That's sweet of you, Carol, but you need a thick skin to run a company. Like I told Mr. Hoffman, it's just business."

"But he said it was his life," I argued.

"Then he should have made his company stronger. You've studied Darwin in school? Survival of the fittest?" We nodded. "That's the business world. Only the strong survive. It's a cold hard fact, but that's reality. Now, girls, I really must get back to work."

"OK," we both said. I understood what my uncle was saying and how society was based on competition and all that, but I still felt sad for the little man and his lost, little company. "Can I ask one more thing?"

"Goodness, Carol. What is it?" Impatience dripped from his voice.

"What does his company make?"

My uncle paused, and then his granite face hardened into a smirk. "You mean *my* company." A chill crept up my spine. "Baby dolls," he said and turned back to his laptop.

Million-dollar companies, hostile takeovers, angry business owners, ruthless negotiations, all over baby dolls. My uncle, it was safe to say, was no Santa Claus.

Mr. Winters and I stood inside the giant freezer in the school kitchen, our breath puffing out like smoke from a steam engine. I shivered, though that was mostly in my mind. I actually wasn't cold, just freaked out that my training involved standing in a freezer, closing my eyes and "powering up," as Mr. Winters called it.

It had been only a day since we returned from New York (Amelia and I got an A+ on our project!), and my training had already begun. Mr. Winters hadn't wasted any time, calling my uncle Monday evening and talking him into allowing me to start staying after school for forty-five minutes of "tutoring," supposedly with two other kids. "OK, I fibbed about the other kids," Mr. Winters said, "but not about tutoring. It's just not math like I told him." Uncle Christopher agreed to Mondays through Thursdays, when Gus picked me up, but not Friday, when he did. "Carol, dear, my schedule is very strict." So there we were Tuesday, in the freezer, "powering up."

"What does that mean?" I asked.

"You and I are made for the cold. We draw power from it."

"So I can just stick my head in a fridge and become all powerful and stuff?"

Mr. Winters laughed. "Not exactly, dear heart. In fact, this isn't ideal. Artificial cold is not pure. But it's all we have, so we'll make do."

"So if we were in snow and ice and cold, we'd get stronger?"

"Exactly. Why do you think Santa lives at the North Pole? His power is strongest there, as is ours. We don't live there all year round like he does—just for a couple of weeks before Christmas to power up so we can do our jobs." I thought back to my father. I was too young then to really remember, but I felt pretty certain I'd never been to the North Pole. So had he gone up there by himself every year? I remembered him being home on Christmas morning, especially the year my parents gave me the carved Santa, so he must have finished his duties in time to get back. Now that I was training to be a Defender, did that mean I'd be at the North Pole every Christmas? For the rest of my life? And what would I do up there? It was all so weird to think about.

"What's the power for?" I asked.

"Goodness, m'lady. I thought you would have figured that out by now. We help Santa slow time to be able to make all his deliveries in one night. But with fewer Defenders and more and more children, it's getting tougher to complete his mission."

"How are you so sure I have this power?"

"First off, it tends to run in families. And think about it, m'lady. The day you touched the reindeer, it was probably eighty-five degrees. So with no cold, no training, and no knowledge of your ability, you sent that animal skyward. You filled it with the Christmas magic that lives inside you. It was miraculous."

I sure hadn't felt miraculous that day. I felt more like the idiot who destroyed the holiday festival and sent a hot-air balloon on a fifty-mile journey that ended with it landing on someone's house and making the local news. "So what do we do?" I asked.

Mr. Winters took my hands. His hair was black again, instead of red with the white stripe. ("A little magical dye," he explained.) "Close your eyes," he said. I did, feeling unbelievably stupid. "Do you sense the power?"

I concentrated, trying to feel what Mr. Winters wanted me to feel. "Um, sort of," I lied. Other than the warmth from his fingers, I sensed nothing.

"Now open yourself up. Let that power flow into every pore. You did it in New York. When the snow started falling, I saw you transform. Your body knew you were in your element, even if your mind didn't."

"OK," I said, thinking back to the moment when those beautiful flakes touched my tongue and how alive that made me feel.

"Open every pore to the power of the cold," Mr. Winters continued. I closed my eyes and scrunched my face in concentration. But nothing happened. I don't know about you, but I can't control my pores. Not a single one. They seem to handle themselves fine on their own without me meddling in their affairs. I opened my eyes to see Mr. Winters just inches from my face, his eyes wide and staring. I screamed and jumped back. "Good gravy, Mr. Winters! Don't do that!"

"I was watching you."

"Two inches from my face?"

"I'm sorry, m'lady." He glanced at his watch. "Looks like we have to go."

"Just stop time."

"Our powers are not to be wielded unless absolutely necessary."

"Oh," I answered, a little disappointed. Seeing everything come to a halt was pretty darn cool. "I'm sorry I couldn't open my pores, Mr. Winters. I tried."

He laughed. "That's OK, m'lady. It will come. You just need to trust what's within you."

He opened the freezer door, peeked to make sure

no one was around, and hurried out. Gus would be waiting.

Two more days of training and nothing. Zilch. No power, not even a hint of stopping time or the Christmas magic I supposedly had in me. "You're trying too hard, m'lady," Mr. Winters said.

"How can a person try too hard?"

"You're tense. You need to just let go and trust what's within you."

"Maybe it's not within me," I responded, feeling more and more depressed. "Maybe the reindeer was just a fluke."

I could see sympathy in Mr. Winters's eyes, and I didn't like it one bit. I wanted to be strong, to be a Defender. When they had first asked, I wasn't so sure. But the more we trained and the more I thought about the person I would eventually become, the more it mattered that Mr. Winters and Santa thought I was special. I didn't want to let them down. But here I was, not opening my pores, not stopping time, not finding the power I supposedly had so much of. Here I was just being plain old ordinary Carol Glover. "Maybe we've asked too much of you, dear heart," Mr. Winters said. "Take the weekend and recharge." I nodded, afraid I'd cry if I spoke. Mr. Winters gave my shoulder a squeeze. He opened the freezer door and ushered me out. "We'll try again Monday."

On the way home, in the back of the limo, I'll admit it, I moped, feeling sorry for myself. Gus looked at me in the rearview mirror. "What's wrong, squirt?" He had called me that for as long as I could remember. I liked it, though I pretended not to, being almost a grown woman and all.

"Nothing," I mumbled. Gus is a great guy. He's huge, as a bodyguard/chauffeur for a powerful businessman should be, but he's really just a big, cuddly teddy bear. He always asks how my day went. He likes to tease me about boys, which, considering the fact that I find most boys totally gross, gives him a lot of material. He's always there to listen. And on days when I'm "in a mood," as he puts it, he'll stop for something he knows I love but the Voice of Reason never lets me have. ("Carol, dear, it's not healthy.") Ice cream. I *love* ice cream. Maybe it's the cold thing and my secret powers and all that, but I suspect it's mostly because ICE CREAM TASTES AMAZ-A-LICIOUS! So when it was clear I was "in a mood" after my failed training, Gus said, "I know what you need."

"That's OK. Let's just go home." Sometimes a girl just wants to be miserable.

"Nonsense. When have you ever turned down chocolate chip?"

"I'm not hungry," I responded, wallowing in my own crankiness.

"Too bad, squirt," Gus said. "If you don't want any, then you can watch me eat. I need some sugary goodness."

I crossed my arms and stuck out my bottom lip. I just wanted to go to my outlandishly decorated room, flip on the TV, and pout. Gus pulled into our favorite spot, the Malt Shop, a restaurant designed like a 1950s burger joint. It had a black-and-white checkerboard floor, candy-apple-red seats, an old-timey jukebox, and waitresses who zipped around on roller skates in their poodle skirts and bobby socks. Elvis Presley's "Blue Christmas" was playing when we walked in. Boy, did that ever match my mood.

"Two chocolate chip ice creams, please," Gus said to the teenager at the counter. I was going to object, keep the whole crankiness thing going, but I decided to keep quiet. For Gus's sake, naturally. I could tell he *really* wanted that ice cream. I'm nothing if not generous. The boy handed me my cone. I licked the chocolate chip ice cream and shuddered with delight. I followed Gus out the door, trying hard not to show how much I was enjoying the treat. "We're a little behind schedule, squirt," he said. "We'll eat on the way home." My uncle would be annoyed if we came in late, especially if it was because we stopped for ice cream. Gus was taking a risk doing this.

He opened the limo door, and I smiled at him. He had ice cream in his mustache and grinned back at me. Suddenly, I heard a shriek. Gus whipped his head around. A woman screamed, running across the parking lot toward the street. Ahead of her ran a little boy, maybe four years old, chasing a balloon being blown by the breeze. "Tommy, no!" the mother shouted. But the boy was determined to catch that balloon. Across the parking lot he ran, faster than I could have imagined possible for such a tiny thing. He neared the lot exit, the balloon almost in the street. Cars zipped by. Gus took off. The mother screamed again for her son to stop. But all he saw was his balloon. No one would be able to reach him if he didn't stop on his own. The balloon blew into the street, bouncing along the blacktop. An SUV came barreling through and just missed it, the wind yanking the balloon into the path of traffic coming the other direction. The boy ran into the road. A pickup truck headed right for him. The mother screamed. The driver slammed on his brakes. Tires squealed.

I watched in horror. My hand clenched so hard that I crushed the cone, the ice cream toppling to the pavement. I closed my eyes, not wanting to see what was about to happen. Something stirred inside me. I heard another scream and realized it was my own. Then there was silence. No, that's not right. The sound was distorted. I waited for the thump of truck on tiny body, but it never came, just that weird sound. I opened my eyes and was shocked to see that everything was moving in slow motion. Gus still ran toward the child. The mother still screamed. The balloon bounced across the road. And the pickup still headed directly toward that little boy. But all super slowly.

I dropped the remains of my cone and sprinted past Gus. I ran in front of the mother, glancing up to see the terror in her face. I leaped into the street. The truck's bumper was only inches from the boy and still coming, slowly, but just as deadly. I grabbed the boy, turned, and dove with him back to the grass along the road. My knee banged the concrete curb. The pain was enough to break whatever spell I'd cast, and everything sped up again. The truck slid by us. The drivers behind him hit their brakes. Horns blared. Bumpers crunched. The mother reached us a second later and yanked the boy from my arms, sobbing and squeezing him hard. The boy screamed but appeared unhurt. Gus ran up beside me. "Are you all right?"

My knee throbbed. Blood soaked through my pant leg. I nodded. It hurt like the dickens, but it was only a bad scrape. I could see it through the hole in my khakis.

"How did you . . . ?" Gus looked back toward the limo, then at the street, then at me. "You were behind me," he said, and then he noticed my bloody knee. "Are you sure you're OK, squirt?"

"I'm fine," I said. Gus helped me up. The mother of the boy nearly tackled me. She pulled me tight against her chest with her left arm, the little boy gripped in her right. He wailed in my ear. "Thank you! Thank you! Thank you!" the mother repeated over and over.

"You're welcome, ma'am," I squeaked out, trying hard to breathe.

People were jumping out of vehicles. The man in the pickup ran over to us. *"Ay dios mio,"* he said, looking to the sky and clasping his hands together like he was praying. "I so sorry. I so sorry."

The mother smiled at him. "It's OK. Everybody's OK." I heard a far-off siren. An ambulance? The police? I realized I'd have to answer questions. What would I say? I couldn't tell them the truth, that I had slowed down time to save the little boy. I couldn't tell them that there was power within me. I couldn't tell them that after what I thought was useless training, my pores were wide open.

CHAPTER 5

I Hear Humming

I couldn't sleep that night, which I guess isn't surprising. I mean, it's not every day a girl like me stops time and saves a kid's life. I spent half the night staring at the ceiling, listening to the grandfather clock down the hall tick the hours away. I replayed the day's events over and over in my mind. The near tragedy. Gus staring at me with such a puzzled look. The police officer asking questions. The EMT bandaging my knee. My uncle appearing at the scene, studying me as curiously as Gus had, as if he didn't know me. Mr. Winters showing up but standing off in the distance. I waved, but he turned and walked away. I wondered if he'd be mad. Maybe I had violated some

Defenders code, using my power that way. But surely Santa would want me to save a child?

All that aside, something else kept me awake. When my mind finally began to settle and I started to drift off, I heard humming. Faint at first, then louder. It wasn't any tune I recognized, but definitely a song. I thought maybe it was coming from inside the house, but knew it couldn't be my uncle. He's the last person on Earth to be humming. I also knew it couldn't be any of the staff, because they wouldn't risk annoying the boss. And when I'd sit up to listen more closely, the humming would disappear. That kept me up half the night, and, finally, out of pure exhaustion, I drifted off to sleep. I awoke at 7:00 a.m., bleary-eyed, the humming gone. I wondered if I was losing my mind.

I wanted to talk to Mr. Winters but would have to wait till the end of the day. And even then, I'd have only a few minutes. It was Friday, the day my uncle picked me up. During class I caught Mr. Winters staring at me a couple of times with a worried expression. He seemed distracted, not his usual jolly, weird self. He hadn't even been reading under his desk when we arrived. Just sitting in the chair like a normal teacher, which made me worry even more. Maybe Defenders swore an oath to never use their powers to interfere with real life. Maybe it would mess up the future or something. I still had so much to learn about my power.

Finally, the day ended, and I hung around, waiting for my classmates to leave. After Mr. Winters watched the last kid go—it was Amelia, who I'd barely talked to all day, so lost in my own thoughts—he opened his mouth as if to say something, then closed it again. I'd never seen the man at a loss for words and that scared the daylights out of me.

"Am I in trouble?" I asked.

Mr. Winters had a pained look. "Of course not, dear heart. It's just . . ." He shook his head. "How did you do that?"

"You've been training me. Maybe it stuck."

"But none of us could do anything like that so soon. It takes years."

I shrugged. "I just did it. How did you know, anyway?"

"Defenders sense any nearby use of our power," Mr. Winters explained. "It was like an earthquake hit when you did that. Tell me how you felt right before it happened."

"Scared, I guess. I thought I was going to see that little boy die."

"And what did you do?"

"I closed my eyes and screamed."

Mr. Winters gasped. "Oh, my goodness."

"What?" I asked, not liking where the conversation was heading. I thought he would reassure me, not make me feel worse.

"You have more power than we imagined, Carol," Mr. Winters said. "But I fear that if you're not careful, it could overwhelm you."

"I don't understand."

Mr. Winters sighed. "It appears your power is not only fueled by the cold and innate ability, like the rest of us Defenders, but also by emotion."

"And that's bad?"

"Maybe. The older you get, the more powerful you'll get, and if you lose your temper or get scared, like when you saw that boy, your ability could consume you."

"Consume? Like explode or something?"

"I don't know. It happened once long before I was a Defender. Santa won't talk about it. But a Defender lost control and simply vanished into thin air." Mr. Winters made a gesture with his right hand, flicking his fingers open. "Poof."

A lump formed in the back of my throat. "But I'll learn to control it," I insisted. "You can help me."

"I hope so, dear heart. But soon you may be beyond what I know."

"What do you mean?"

Mr. Winters thought for a moment. "I'm pretty good at math and can teach it well. But if Einstein needed help with his theory of relativity, I sure wouldn't be the one to ask." I heard footsteps down the hall, hurrying footsteps. "We'll have to continue this later, dear heart. Don't worry yourself too much."

Don't worry? The guy says I might disappear if I don't learn to control my power and he tells me not to worry! Sheesh. "There's one more thing," I said. "I'm hearing humming at night, like a song."

Mr. Winters's eyes grew wide. "What?"

"Humming," I repeated. The footsteps grew louder.

"Oh, my goodness," Mr. Winters said. I felt a pang of fear. Why did he react that way? But my uncle stood at the door.

"My apologies, kind sir," Mr. Winters said, leaping from his seat, suddenly back to his weird self. "Do not fault your precious charge for her tardiness. We were discussing math difficulties."

"Yes, well, thank you for your diligence, Mr. Winters. But I must insist that on Fridays you do not delay my niece again."

"Of course, of course," Mr. Winters said jovially. He was once again shaking my uncle's hand so vigorously that both their bodies bounced. "My deepest apologies." Mr. Winters winked and gave me a reassuring smile. It didn't make me feel any better.

I heard the humming at night again that weekend. I thought I was going crazy. In some ways, it was almost soothing, like a mother humming to her child. But it's hard to feel soothed when you hear humming and no one else is in the room. All you feel is bonkers. I even turned on the lamp suddenly, as if there might be a twisted serial hummer on the loose, sneaking into kids' rooms at night to hum his crazy songs, and I might catch him in the act. But there was nothing, no one. I was desperate to talk to Mr. Winters, to find out why he reacted the way he did. I asked Gus to take me to school early on Monday. But when I arrived, there was no Mr. Winters. "Out sick," according to the substitute teacher, a frightening-looking old woman with a giant mole on the tip of her nose that made it look like her body was trying to grow more nose.

"Do you know when he'll be back?" I asked, frantic. We were only two weeks away from Christmas, so maybe he had to report to the North Pole. But surely Mr. Winters wouldn't just leave without some sort of explanation, without saying goodbye. How could he just abandon me like that?

"I'm sure I wouldn't know, young lady," she snapped, the mole seeming to quiver on the end of her nose. "I'm not psychic." *Psycho* maybe, I thought, probably unfairly. But she didn't need to be so hateful. And she was just as nasty the rest of the day. After a weekend of no sleep and worrying I was losing my mind, and now panicked about Mr. Winters's abrupt disappearance, I'd had enough. When I sneezed and the teacher yelled, "Quiet!" I snapped. Let's just say it was not my finest moment.

"I can't help sneezing, you Old Mole Nose!" I yelled. And I slammed my fist on my desk in a rage. What I said was terrible enough, but that wasn't the worst of it. Hitting my desk created a weird air disturbance, like some sort of invisible wave. The blast knocked Old Mole Nose backward on her rolling chair, and she slammed into the chalkboard. The pull-down map snapped upward. And when it did, the map string caught the back of her hair and yanked it off her head. She wore a wig! Amelia put her hand to her mouth in shock. Most of the class was too stunned to laugh. Except Vincent, of course. He cackled and whispered, "You're in for it now, Christmas Carol." Old Mole Nose felt the top of her bare head. She shrieked, leaping out of her chair and pointing at the door. "Principal's office, young lady! I'll have you suspended. I don't care who your uncle is."

I wasn't angry anymore. I was frightened. I could have really hurt her. Was this the power Mr. Winters worried would consume me? I gathered up my books and walked, in silence, out of the classroom. I didn't want to look at Old Mole Nose, or Amelia, or anyone else. I didn't want to go home and face my uncle. I didn't want to be a Defender and have these strange powers I couldn't control. I didn't want to be who I apparently was. I needed to talk to someone. I needed a friend. And I'd been so distracted by all that was happening to me, I realized I'd neglected Amelia for the past week. I hadn't once invited her to my house after school. And at lunch that day, I'd practically ignored her, so much so that Amelia snapped, "If you're going to be such a gloomy stick-in-the-mud, I'll find better company." So the one person who could make me feel better had stormed off.

Walking down the empty hallway toward the principal's office, feeling miserable and more alone than I ever had, I looked up. Standing in front of me, silhouetted against the light from the front windows, stood Mr. Winters, the person I feared had abandoned me. I stopped. I wanted to be angry with him for not being there that day when I needed him most. But I was so relieved that I ran to hug him. Before I could, however, he stopped me with the look

CHAPTER 6

Making a Pole Vault

I barfed the first time we made the "Pole vault." That's
what Mr. Winters called our trip to the North Pole. I still
don't get how it works. Something about bending time
and space, the curvature of the earth, traveling a straight
line instead of along a curve. Whatever. It made me puke.

We executed the Pole vault behind Broward Academy,
out of sight of any witnesses. Mr. Winters took my hands
and said, "Hold on!" I closed my eyes, opened them
briefly to see the world around me stretched and bent
all at the same time, closed them once more, and then
when I opened my eyes again, we were standing at the
North Pole. I immediately deposited the remains of my
fish stick/tater tot/green bean school lunch in the snow.

Lovely. Mr. Winters patted me gently on the back as I bent over. "Happens to all of us, dear heart."

I wiped my mouth and looked around. Snow covered everything, weighing down the green pines, piled high on every building, burying mysterious objects that formed large lumps in the landscape. We stood in front of a huge log house, plainly built, but inviting. A soft light glowed in the windows. A pine wreath with red ribbons hung on the front door. A mailbox with the name CLAUS stenciled in red letters stood at the end of a walkway to the house. I wondered who in the world delivered Santa's mail; I'd have to ask about that later.

To our left stood a giant structure that looked like a barn. The snow was trampled in front, and I wondered if that was where the reindeer lived. It was bitter cold. My breath steamed in front of me. But just like in New York, it didn't bother me much, even though I wore only a red, short-sleeved shirt and white pants. As I watched Mr. Winters approach the front door, my heart raced. I couldn't believe it. I was standing at the North Pole! Where Santa Claus lives! His house looked just like I'd imagined, all homey and welcoming, as if its doors would open to anyone. But did I truly belong here? I felt paralyzed, nervous, even a little frightened.

"Come inside, m'lady," Mr. Winters called. The sound of his voice made me jump, and suddenly it was as if someone had started a movie in my brain. The snow, the cold, those words—they triggered something. I heard my mother's voice calling from the front door of our snow-covered house in Syracuse, "Come inside, Carol!" I remembered Dad running past Mom and stomping through the deep snow, scooping me up and laughing, my mother just shaking her head and going back into the house. "You see that, Angel Butt? Mean old Mommy wants us to go inside." And I smiled, remembering the silly nickname my father always called me. I remembered the two of us making snow angels and Dad shaking the snow out of his white-streaked red hair, the hair I now knew signified what he was. We stared up at the gray sky, knowing Mom would have two cups of steaming hot chocolate inside, marshmallows floating like tiny buoys. I remembered tearing into my gifts on Christmas morning, opening the package with the beautifully carved wooden Santa, while my parents watched and smiled. I remembered setting that

Santa on the table next to my bed, looking at it every night before I fell asleep. I remembered what it was like to be five and feel safe and have two people love you more than anything in the world. It all came back to me in a rush, and my eyes welled with tears. Mr. Winters looked at me. "Are you OK, m'lady?"

I nodded, pushing aside the memory, knowing it would always be there for me to revisit. I wished I had my wooden Santa, the only thing I had left of my parents, other than memory, but it sat on the dresser in my room in Hillsboro. Maybe someday I could go back and get it. Mr. Winters opened the front door, and I stepped inside, the warmth washing over me. I wiped my eyes. My legs felt wobbly. "Is Santa's workshop here, too?" I asked. I could hardly breathe from the excitement.

Mr. Winters chuckled. "No, dear heart, just his house. He doesn't really have a workshop nowadays. You'll see." The house was even bigger than it appeared from outside. Everything was made of polished red wood. The floors gleamed so brightly our reflections shone back at us, and I had the urge to kick off my shoes and slide across the floor in my socks. A roaring fire crackled and popped in the hearth. Stockings were hung by the chimney. (With care, I suppose.) A Santa house music box tinkled the tune "Here Comes Santa Claus." A huge Christmas tree weighed down with decorations sparkled in the corner. Gifts covered every inch of space under the tree. Wonderful smells wafted from the kitchen. Turkey, I guessed. Maybe mashed potatoes and gravy, pumpkin pie. My now-empty stomach rumbled.

Along the far wall was perhaps the coolest thing I'd ever seen. The whole wall—probably thirty feet wide and ten feet high—was a bookshelf covered with clear glass, sort of like a museum display. And when I thought about it, that's exactly what it was. A display on the history of toys! I wandered over and realized that these weren't just ordinary toys but the best of the best from decades, even centuries, past. Starting on the top shelf were the earliest toys: ancient-looking rag dolls made from cloth and straw, small carved stone figures, wooden building blocks, a tattered stuffed bear, a tiny wooden wagon, baby rattles. The next shelf held colorful tin toys, marbles, a ball and jacks, a small bucket and shovel, a baseball bat and odd-looking leather glove, elaborate dolls with beautiful eyes, wooden soldiers, and a Radio Flyer wagon. The next shelf displayed more modern treasures, some still in their original boxes: electric trains, a windup Mickey Mouse metal figure, board games like checkers and Monopoly, a ray gun, some kind of doll called "Howdy Doody." Each shelf held newer and newer toys: Barbies, G.I. Joes, an Easy-Bake Oven, Mr. Potato Heads, Cabbage Patch dolls, a Slinky, Beanie Babies, remote control cars, Legos, video games, until, at last, on the very bottom, sat iPads, ZhuZhu pets, Xbox and Wii, and the hottest toy of the current holiday season (one I'd heard my uncle complaining about because it wasn't made by his company): a My Pretty Beatrice doll that had red hair, like mine. I was too old for dolls, but that didn't stop me from wanting to hug her tight to my chest. There was something wonderful about the feel of a beautiful doll.

I heard footsteps and turned, noticing for the first time a spiral staircase. Down the stairs came two big feet in white socks. Then bright red pants, a red sweater lined with white, and, last, the pudgy face with its full, white beard. He wasn't wearing his hat, but it was the man himself. I honestly thought I might explode with happiness.

"Welcome, Carol," Santa said as he stepped off the staircase. "I trust you had a good journey." And he laughed. Not a ho-ho-ho. Just a normal old guy laugh. But filled with joy and warmth. I was pretty sure Santa was poking fun at me—probably knowing I puked—but with that laugh, I didn't mind. His belly even shook a little, though I wouldn't describe it as a bowl full of jelly. Who puts jelly in a bowl, anyway? That's what jars are for!

I nodded. I wanted to ask about the toys but was too intimidated to speak. Santa glanced at Mr. Winters, and his smile vanished. He looked my way again, studying me. I shifted nervously, like a little kid who has to pee, which, come to think of it, I actually did. "So," Santa said at last, "tell me about the humming."

That surprised me. I expected him to ask about the little boy. I still thought I might be in trouble. "I hear humming," I said, then realized how dumb that sounded. That's what the man just said!

But Santa simply smiled. "Yes, sweetheart," he said gently. "Tell me more. Give me whatever details you can."

I thought about it, trying to find the words. "It's gotten stronger the past two nights. Or louder. Or clearer. Or whatever."

"I see," Santa said, tugging thoughtfully at his beard. I wondered where Mrs. Claus was, or if there even was a Mrs. Claus. Maybe Santa was a bachelor. "And it's a tune, you say. A song."

"Not one I recognize, but, yes, the same song repeats over and over." I thought for a second, trying to hear the song in my memory. I hummed the notes: a simple tune that went up, then down, slowly at first, then up and down more quickly, then down, down, down. Santa and Mr. Winters gasped.

"That's the song you hear?" Mr. Winters asked. He was suddenly standing next to me, his face bright with anticipation.

"Yes," I said. "What is it?"

"It's good news, m'lady," Mr. Winters said. "It means a Defender we thought lost is still alive."

"I don't get it."

"It's like a distress signal," Santa explained. "But for years, we've had no one capable of picking it up." Mr.

Winters hummed the rest of the tune back to me and gooseflesh sprang up on my arms. He knew the song! Something I thought was only in my head!

"Who's humming it?" I asked.

"We don't know," Santa said. "Half of our number has disappeared. A few may have left on their own. Others, we fear, met a nefarious end. But we've always held out hope that some are out there waiting for us to rescue them." A flicker of a thought crossed my mind, though I didn't dare say it aloud. But Santa knew. Of course he knew. "Yes, sweetheart, maybe your father." Santa looked away, as if trying to gather himself. I thought he might cry. "He was a fine man."

I nodded, a tear trickling down my cheek. *You* try not crying when Santa's all sad and emotional right in front of you. I wiped the tear away, hoping they hadn't seen. I wanted to ask how we could use the humming to find the missing Defender. Was it truly possible I could get my father back? For that, I would do anything. But a voice called out from the back, a female voice. "Kris, dinnertime!" I looked at my watch. Six o'clock! It had been early afternoon when we left Broward. How could time have passed so quickly?

A woman emerged from the kitchen. She had long, silver hair that shone like it had been polished. Her cheeks were rosy, and her skin was as smooth and beautiful as porcelain. She was tall and slender and striking, like a fashion model in her later years. She wore a simple, white housedress and had a bright red apron tied around her waist. When she saw me, her face lit up and she rushed across the room. She moved with such grace it was as if she flew, hovering just above the floor. She wasn't at all what I had pictured, but I knew without a doubt that this was Mrs. Claus. "Oh, my sweet dear," she whispered and pulled me into such a fierce hug it took my breath away. She was warm and soft and smelled of pine, making me think of the wonderful aroma of the Rockefeller Christmas tree. "Welcome to our home."

"Carol, this is Mrs. Claus," Santa said. "The *real* boss."

Mrs. Claus pulled away and smiled, her blue eyes twinkling. "That's right, Carol. He'd be lost without me." She winked at Santa, and he threw back his head and laughed. She put her arm around my shoulder and pulled me toward the wondrous smells in the back. "That's enough business for now," Mrs. Claus declared. "The girl must eat." Santa started to say something but simply shrugged and followed us to dinner. The boss had spoken.

That night Santa sat right outside my door while I tried to sleep, and if you want to know the truth, it freaked me out a little. Actually, it freaked me out a lot. *You* try sleeping while Santa Claus listens to you snore. "A necessary evil, dear heart," Mr. Winters explained after dinner. I was so stuffed with turkey, mashed potatoes, green beans, buttered rolls, and pumpkin pie that I could barely move. I had offered to help with the dishes, but Mrs. Claus just smiled warmly. "So sweet of you, dear, but the elves will take care of that." Elves? I wanted to see elves! But Mr. Winters was already pulling me back out to the living room where we were to discuss the "business" Mrs. Claus had delayed. "Remember how I said the Defenders help power Santa's magic?" Mr. Winters asked. "Well, it works the other way, too. His magic focuses our power, like a wire conducts electricity."

"But what's he going to do?" I asked as I sipped a mug

of warm apple cider. It was so delicious I could hardly focus on what Mr. Winters was saying.

"Don't worry. It won't hurt," he said. "He just taps into your mind to hear the Defender's distress call. Hopefully he can pinpoint where it's coming from."

So Santa sat outside my door as I lay in bed staring at the ceiling. I had been given a small room, very cozy, with a single bed, a small chest, and a bookshelf filled with leather-bound books that looked as old as I imagined Santa to be. A candle burned atop the chest. Shadows played on the walls. "You have to sleep, dear," Santa said, peeking in. "That opens your mind to the tune." Easier said than done with you sitting there listening to me, I wanted to say. But I just tried to clear my mind. I truly was exhausted. My body felt like a washrag that had been wrung dry. "From the Pole vault," Mr. Winters explained. "Perfectly natural."

But sometimes you're so tired you can't sleep. I tossed and turned. I buried my face in the pillow, periodically flipping it over to the cool side. I counted sheep, getting to 1,132 when I decided that wasn't going to work either. My left leg shook nervously. I thought about my uncle and the note Mr. Winters said he mailed, telling him I was safe, and how my uncle probably wouldn't believe it and would have the police searching for me. I thought about my father and whether he might actually be alive. I worried about what Santa and Mr. Winters were asking me to do and whether I would let them down. Maybe I wasn't cut out to be a Defender. I heard Santa clear his throat lightly. I suspected he was getting impatient, and that made me all the more nervous. Then I heard humming. I got excited until I realized it was Santa, not the voice in my head. He started out with the tune I'd heard, softly humming the peculiar notes. The song was a little creepy but stuck in my brain all the same, like a weird pop hit. When Santa was done with that, he started with Christmas songs. "Silver Bells." "White Christmas." He had a pleasant voice, soft and soothing. "O Christmas Tree." "Joy to the World." I felt myself getting drowsy.

I was so very tired, more tired than I'd ever been. I heard the odd tune once more, growing stronger, and at first I thought it was Santa again. Then I realized it was in my head. A different voice. I concentrated hard, pulling the song toward me. I could hear it as clearly as if the

CHAPTER 7

Sabana Grande de Palenque

We stood in a circle, holding hands. Santa, me, Mr. Winters, and the rest of the Defenders, who came from around the world. Looking at them, I realized they all had two things in common: they were all adults, and each had bright red hair with a streak of white. "It's like a red-haired United Nations," Mr. Winters joked. There was Nori Takahari from Japan, a small, intense-looking man with coal black eyes who bowed when Santa introduced us. Next up was Chidi Yakubu, a Nigerian with a musical accent that tickled my ears, then Gerta Kaufmann, a German woman with piercing blue eyes. The others were Toby Wise from

Australia, Natasha Andropov from Russia, Samantha Blair from the United Kingdom, Tomas Martinez from Chile, and Thulie Botha from South Africa.

Last was a guy from my best friend's home country: the Dominican Republic. His name was Ramon Trinidad, and he was tall and slender and moved with a grace that reminded me of Mrs. Claus. His smile was unlike any I'd ever seen, unless you count movie stars, and I'd never seen one of those in person. He had the whitest, most perfect teeth in the history of teeth, whiter than the streak in his own red hair. When Santa introduced us, Ramon smiled and bowed low. My face flushed and I stuttered, "N-n-n-nice to meet you." He smiled again and my knees wobbled. Good gravy, what was wrong with me? I could be such a weirdo.

"It appears we'll be visiting Ramon's home," Santa said.

"You will love it, Carol," Ramon said. "My country is beautiful. I will show you the beaches and the mountains, and the people will welcome you with open arms." I hardly heard a word. I couldn't stop staring at that smile. I was too tongue-tied to even tell him that my best friend was Dominican.

"We won't have time for sightseeing," Santa said and motioned for us to gather around. It was early morning but still dark. "Take hands and form a circle." The Defenders did as Santa asked, stretching their arms to full length and closing their eyes. Ramon stood on my left and Mr. Winters on my right. I felt a tingle in my fingers, like the electric charge when I'd touched that reindeer. I instinctively pulled away, afraid I was about to get a shock. But Mr. Winters and Ramon tightened their grips. The tingle increased until there was a steady hum, like a power line. I felt a surge in my chest. My hair felt like it was lifting off of my scalp. I'd never felt better. It was like when I was on the ice at Rockefeller Center but ten times more exhilarating. At last, the Defenders let go. Ramon turned to me with eyes wide and whispered, "You have great power within you, *mi'ja*." So everyone keeps telling me, I wanted to say.

I heard a racket behind me and turned to see what was going on. Snow had begun to fall, but through the flakes I watched the huge doors to the barn swing open. Out came eight reindeer, pulling Santa's massive sleigh. Behind them came more reindeer, and on the back of those were the most beautiful creatures I'd ever seen. They weren't dwarflike, but slight, like wood pixies in a fairy tale, and about my height. These had to be the elves! At last! I had the strange urge to run up and hug them, but I managed to restrain myself. They'd probably think I was some kind of weirdo.

Each elf held the reins of the reindeer it rode, and when a Defender approached, the elf would leap from the back of the beast, almost floating to the ground. They wore fur-lined suits of red, and little green shoes that looked like moccasins. Their hair was thick and long and snow-white, their pointy ears emerging through the flowing white. One rode toward me and smiled. His eyes were silver, his skin pale. He handed me the reins of a massive reindeer that snorted and shook his head. *Welcome, beautiful one.* I heard the words but realized the elf's mouth hadn't moved. "They do not speak," Mr. Winters said. "They communicate with telepathy, and only with each other."

"I heard him," I said.

"You what?"

"He welcomed me." I turned back to the elf. "Thank you so much. It's very nice to meet you."

I am honored to meet the Gifted One, the elf said, and goose-flesh covered my arms. He leaped from the deer, hurrying back to the barn. As he ran across the snow, I was amazed to see he left no prints. "He called me 'the Gifted One,'" I said to Mr. Winters. "What does that mean?"

"Astonishing, m'lady. I've never heard a word those scrawny devils say. Only Santa can. You do indeed possess special abilities." Mr. Winters lifted me onto the back of the reindeer. He walked over to another deer a few feet away. "Now we must ride."

"I'm riding by myself?" I asked, trying not to panic. I rubbed the reindeer's neck. Even through the gloves Mrs. Claus made me wear, I could feel his powerful muscles as he shifted and rocked like a racehorse in the starting gate.

"Yes, oh Gifted One," Mr. Winters said with a smirk. He jumped onto the back of his deer. "Don't worry, m'lady, I'll ride beside you. Just do this." He slammed his legs against the torso of the deer and yelled, "Haaaa!" The reindeer surged forward, taking just a few strides before it soared into the snowy night sky, making my heart feel as if it might fly right out of my chest. I did as Mr. Winters said, thumping my legs against the deer and meekly saying, "Haaa." The reindeer took off. That's when I remembered I hadn't grabbed the reins. The deer flew forward. I stayed right where I was, tumbling backward into the snow. The fall knocked the breath out of me and I lay on my back, gasping. I stared at the sky as my reindeer flew above me and looked down, surely puzzled why I hadn't joined him. "Make sure you hold onto the reins, m'lady," Mr. Winters called, and he laughed.

"Gee, thanks," I muttered, standing up and brushing snow out of my clothes and hair. I sucked in deep breaths. My reindeer circled around, landing softly next to me. He put his nose in my hand and snorted. I wondered if he was laughing at me. I reached for the reins and jumped onto his back. Only I jumped too hard and slid over the other side. I hung there struggling to pull myself up, feeling ridiculous, until at last I gave up and let myself fall to the ground. My reindeer turned to look at me. He must have thought I was nuts. I stood up and brushed myself off again. "Third time's the charm," I said and jumped on once more. Success! Holding tight this time, I shouted, "Haaa!" and off we flew. Santa's house, the barn, the mysterious lumps in the snow—all of it shrank below me.

Mr. Winters circled around and flew up beside me. I held the reins with all my might, afraid to look down for more than a second.

"Isn't it glorious, m'lady?" Mr. Winters said.

Glorious? I was petrified, gripping the reins so hard my fingers ached. But with my reindeer's legs pumping steadily—the ride as smooth as bicycling through the park—a calm came over me. Snowflakes tickled my cheeks. Santa and the Defenders flew high above. I relaxed and breathed deeply. It *was* glorious.

I glanced down at Santa's. Beyond the house and barn, I saw twinkling lights, many more than the ones shining at Santa's. "What's that?" I shouted, and then realized it was so quiet our voices carried easily.

"Santa's factory," Mr. Winters said.

"Where the elves make the toys?" I asked excitedly. I *soooooo* wanted to visit that factory.

"Some of them," Mr. Winters said. "It's complicated. The world has grown so huge that the elves can no longer meet demand. So Santa relies on suppliers."

"Other people make Santa's toys?" I couldn't believe it. Something seemed wrong about that.

"Yes, m'lady. Santa's just the fulfiller of wishes. Be it by elves or big companies, the toys are made for him."

"I guess," I answered, trying to wrap my mind around that. A thought occurred to me. "What about my uncle's company?"

"I believe so."

"My uncle knows Santa?"

"Of course not, dear heart. None of the companies know they're doing business with Santa. He has representatives who buy on his behalf."

"Oh, I see."

"It's getting more difficult. There are fewer and fewer toy companies and the prices are going up and up. Come to think of it, Santa had to drop your uncle's company last year. His prices were too high, and big companies like his have pushed out the humble, little toy makers."

"That's sad," I said, thinking of the angry man who had confronted my uncle about the doll company International Toy had swallowed like a morsel of food.

"You don't know the half of it, dear heart. These are troubling times."

"How does Santa pay for the toys?"

Mr. Winters laughed. "It's not polite to ask about another's finances, m'lady."

"Sorry," I muttered, embarrassed.

"I'm not involved in the SNC. That's the Saint Nicholas Consortium, the business arm of Santa's operation. The African fellow, Chidi, heads that."

As Mr. Winters talked, I began to notice how warm it had gotten. The snow had stopped. I could no longer see my breath. The sun glowed on the horizon, slowly illuminating what lay below. I peered through the gray morning and saw ocean, endless miles of water. Santa and the other Defenders flew in silence. Mr. Winters talked and talked, gesturing dramatically.

"Where are we?" I asked, interrupting.

Mr. Winters looked down. "Approaching the Dominican Republic, m'lady."

"But how? We've been flying for only a few minutes."

"Just another of Santa's powers. A sort of reverse Pole vault but much more elegant."

That was for sure. At least I wasn't puking into the ocean. I hadn't even noticed leaving the North Pole. Ramon, who had been flying at the head of the pack, slowed down and positioned himself between Mr. Winters and me. He motioned to an island in the distance being lit by the sun. "My home." He pointed to the right side and said, "Haiti," then moved his hand to the left. "The Dominican Republic. A shared land. Two vastly different people."

"It's beautiful," I said. As the sun rose, the water sparkled a deep blue. The beaches were a blazing white, almost as bright as snow, and the water lapped gently on the shores. Mountains rose inland, astonishingly green, with clouds that settled on the peaks like gobs of cotton. We passed over a resort, striped umbrellas lining the beach like tiny pinwheels. It was barely breakfast time, but early risers strolled on the sand or took dips in the Atlantic. "Won't they see us?" I asked.

"Santa cloaks our presence," Ramon responded. "I must lead us home now, *mi'ja*." He bolted ahead, and we followed him toward the mountains.

"He seems like a nice man," I said to Mr. Winters.

"Indeed, m'lady. I trust him with my life."

As we soared over the lush tropical forests of the Dominican Republic, I wondered where Amelia's hometown was and thought of how I hadn't been a very good friend lately. I missed her. And now that I was a Defender, maybe that meant I would never return to Hillsboro. Maybe I would lose my best friend forever. The thought made my heart hurt.

Below us roads coiled across the mountains, like ribbons tossed on the ground. Cars and motorcycles wound their way up the steep inclines. A horse pulled a cart, and men, women, and children walked alongside the road. We flew toward a town nestled between two hills, not far from the ocean. We descended slowly, landing in the backyard of a massive mansion on a hillside. "Welcome to *Sabana Grande de Palenque!*" Ramon said.

"You live here?" I asked.

Spreading his arms, he responded, "*Si. Mi casa es su casa.* My home is yours."

We hopped off our reindeer and led them to a large building behind the main house. Inside were troughs filled with water and oats, and the reindeer dug in hungrily. I wondered if they felt the miles we'd traveled or if Santa's magic made it seem as if they'd gone only a short distance. Ramon led us through the yard, toward the house.

The heat was insane. I'm talking inside of an oven. "How can someone from such a hot place be a Defender?" I asked Ramon. "I thought Defenders liked the cold."

He just smiled his gorgeous smile. "You're from Florida, *mi'ja*," Ramon said. "Isn't that hot?"

"Oh, yeah," I responded, feeling stupid. It was still hard to think of myself as a Defender.

"The magic of Christmas is everywhere, I suppose," Ramon said. "I was born different, just like you. And Santa found me."

The inside of the mansion was cool and refreshing, the air-conditioning on full blast. Everything was white, bright, and spotless. A tastefully decorated Christmas tree, covered in white lights and white ornaments, sat glistening in the foyer. A butler approached with a cart that held cups of ice and pitchers of a fruity-looking drink Ramon said was made from mango and papaya. It was the best thing I'd ever tasted, and he laughed when I gulped it down and asked for more. "Certainly, *mi'ja*." Santa and the rest of the Defenders disappeared into another room. Ramon motioned to the butler, who showed me to a room with a huge television. He disappeared for a few minutes, returning with more juice and a plate full of cookies shaped like Santas and reindeer. I heard a soft meow and looked down to see a snow-white kitten staring up at me with pleading eyes as green as mine. I picked up the kitten, which purred and rubbed its face against my cheek. And that's where I sat for the next couple of hours, channel surfing through Spanish-speaking shows, playing with the cat, eating twelve (yes, twelve!) cookies, and sipping a never-ending supply of juice while the Defenders talked and I got more and more annoyed that I hadn't been included.

When at long last Ramon reappeared, the cat had vanished, I could find nothing to watch, and I was bored. "I trust you're doing well, *mi'ja*," Ramon said.

"I'm fine," I snapped. Ramon grimaced ever so slightly, and I felt bad. It wasn't his fault; he had been nothing but a good host. "What's going on?" I asked, trying to be all grown-up and mature and not show my annoyance.

"Our plan is ready," Ramon said. "Tonight we find our lost Defender. Now we must rest."

"But I'm not tired," I said. The thought of sitting around doing nothing till nightfall was enough to make me scream.

Ramon leaned in and whispered, "Neither am I." He glanced toward the room where Santa and the Defenders still talked. "Come with me, *mi'ja*," he whispered. "I will show you where I come from. Quickly now, before Santa objects." And he laughed again. We hurried out the door and down a long path to a huge iron gate. "How did you get so rich?" I asked, then remembered Mr. Winters reprimanding me for being nosy about other people's money.

Ramon laughed and opened the gate. We were at the edge of a small town. "Sugar cane," he answered. "Various other interests. Even toys, with my whole Santa connection, but I sold that company when I got a huge offer. From your uncle's company actually."

"You know my uncle?"

"Not really. We met only during the sale. And if you want the truth, *mi'ja*, I wouldn't have sold it had I known more about him. He laid off workers and raised prices. I'm sorry to say it, but he's ruthless."

"That's OK. I've seen how he does business. He says it's like Darwin."

"Well, I don't think it has to be that way," Ramon said. "I come from very humble beginnings myself. You'll see." We walked into town, which buzzed with activity. A sign read: SABANA GRANDE DE PALENQUE. Young men on mopeds zipped by at dangerous speeds, most of them carrying a passenger on the back. "Taxis," Ramon explained. "Better than walking everywhere, assuming you don't crash into a wall." Small children played in the street. Some were barefoot, and some were dirty. A boy, kindergarten age, came up to us with his hand out, jabbering in Spanish. Ramon flipped him a coin, and the child squealed with delight, running off and yelling, *"Gracias!"*

"There is much poverty in this place. I'm working to change that. I built a new preschool. I pay fair wages for fair work. I do what I can."

The houses were a wild mix of styles and colors, some falling down and others painted brightly and sparkling clean. We stopped in front of one of the well-kept homes. On the left a large window opened to a small store with candy and groceries and magazines. On the right was an attached house. An ancient woman with long, silver hair emerged from the store. "Mama Consuelo," Ramon said, embracing her. He kissed her on each cheek. The old woman pushed him out of the way to get to me, throwing her bony arms around my neck for a hug. She stepped back and took the long locks of my hair in her hands. *"Que linda!"* she said. She focused on the white strands and glanced at Ramon with questioning eyes.

"Carol," Ramon said. "This is Mama Consuelo, my *abuela*. Grandmother."

"Nice to meet you," I said, though I was pretty sure she didn't understand a word. She nodded and smiled, still stroking my hair.

"Tienes hambre? Comer, comer," she said.

Before Ramon could translate, she led me into the house and directly to the dining room table, which held a huge bowl of white rice, meat piled high on a platter, and a crock filled with brown beans. It was as if she had food just sitting there ready for unexpected guests. But then I realized it was lunchtime and also that I was hungry for something other than cookies. People started wandering into the small house: three girls, one about my age and two younger (one reminded me of Amelia, with her beautiful skin); three young men wearing work clothes and sweating in the heat; two women younger than Mama Consuelo, perhaps her daughters. I was kissed on the cheek a dozen times.

Mama Consuelo piled food on a plate and placed it in front of me. *"Chivo,"* she said. "Goat," Ramon translated. I wasn't sure how I felt about that, but didn't want to insult my hosts. I sat at the table, everyone filling their plates and finding a seat wherever they could. More people arrived. The Spanish chatter intensified. There was laughter and warmth. I didn't comprehend a word being said, but I understood this was a kind and generous family. I hesitantly took a bite of *chivo*. Then another. Then a spoonful of rice and beans. Holy moly, that was good. I ate and I ate. Mama Consuelo continually filled my plate until, at last, Ramon said something in Spanish and laughed, stopping his *abuela's* hand as she started to spoon out more rice.

After lunch, we sat in the living room, Ramon chatting with everyone in Spanish and translating for me on occasion. He had an animated discussion with two of the younger men and seemed to question them intensely. I wondered what they were saying but didn't want to interrupt. But something nagged at me throughout the visit. "Why doesn't your family live with you?" I finally asked. "You have such a huge house."

Ramon laughed. "Too stubborn. Believe me, I've tried. Mama Consuelo supported six kids and a bunch of grandkids with that little store and raised them in this house. She won't ever leave."

I noticed a small Christmas tree in the corner, decorated simply, with a few presents underneath. Tinsel was draped across the windowsill. "What's Christmas like here?" I asked, feeling a bit silly as I thought of my own "over the top" room decorations.

"More modest," Ramon said. "We don't go overboard with presents like Americans do. And we don't give gifts on Christmas Day."

"No way!"

"We have Three Kings Day in January when the kids get gifts."

"So Santa doesn't bring Dominican children presents?"

"Oh, he's definitely involved," Ramon said. "He knows different cultures have different customs, so he respects that." Ramon looked at his watch. "Speaking of the Big Guy, *mi'ja*, we'd better get going. He'll be sending out a search party for us."

It took ten minutes to get out of there. My cheek was

kissed a dozen more times. Mama Consuelo touched my hair and smiled. Her daughters did the same. Ramon spoke quietly again to the two young men. Standing outside, they pointed toward a mountain that rose above the town. When, at last, we made it to the street, Ramon was quiet, lost in thought. "What were you guys talking about?" I asked.

"Strange activities on the island. I believe I know where our missing Defender is."

"I thought Santa knew."

"He senses the general area with his magic. But it's like a war, *mi'ja*. You need boots on the ground to find the enemy's hideout. Someone working in the cane fields spotted a blindfolded man being led into those mountains."

"The Defender?" I asked.

"I hope." He thought for a moment. "It's strange that our enemy's prison should be here, so close to me." He shrugged. "Whatever the reason, tonight it ends. We go to the mountain." Ramon was no longer laughing, no longer smiling. I felt a shiver of fear.

"There is a network of caves in the mountain," Ramon explained to the Defenders. "Someone bought the property and fenced off the main entrance. But I know something they don't. I spent my childhood roaming these mountains. There's another way in." I didn't hear anything more about the plans because they disappeared into that room again. When they were done, Santa and Ramon assigned each Defender a task. Poor Mr. Winters got stuck babysitting me. "I don't mind, m'lady," he insisted, but I didn't believe him.

It was dark when we left the *"Casa de Trinidad,"* as Ramon called his mansion. We lifted off into the night sky, the reindeer pumping their legs in perfect unison, something I hadn't noticed the first trip. "They're connected by Santa's magic," Mr. Winters explained. "When they work as one, they're stronger. Like us."

I nodded, my stomach a twisted knot of nerves. I still wasn't told the details of the plan, because Mr. Winters said Santa insisted I stay back, out of harm's way. "We just want you to observe, dear heart," Mr. Winters said. "We know you can't control your powers yet." Mr. Winters didn't seem concerned about the mission. "We have the element of surprise, and we have numbers. It will be fine."

We approached the mountain where the suspicious activity had been observed. I could make out a complex of gray buildings, surrounded by a chain-link fence with barbed wire ringing the top. A dog barked twice, then went silent. We flew past the fenced-in property and landed in a clearing about a mile away. A full moon gave the landscape a ghostly glow. The Defenders dismounted and the reindeer put their heads down and grazed. Mr. Winters led me to the sleigh where Ramon and the Big Guy talked quietly.

"There's a path up to the secret entrance," Ramon said. "I will lead the way."

Santa turned to Mr. Winters and me. "We'll be back in a flash."

"Why can't we go?" I asked. "I can help." Which, of course, probably wasn't true. It was more likely I'd just get in the way.

"We need someone to take care of the reindeer," Santa said. "That's how we make our escape."

"OK," I said glumly.

"Your time will come, dear," Santa said. "I expect big things from you someday." He turned and whispered sharply to the Defenders. "Off we go!"

"We shall return, *mi'ja*. I promise," Ramon whispered. He hurried into the thick trees, disappearing in an instant. Santa and the rest of the Defenders followed. It was just me and Mr. Winters and the reindeer.

Mr. Winters climbed into the sleigh and sat down, with a thump. I could tell he was about as unhappy as I was to be left behind. I jumped up beside him, and we sat in silence. Animal noises unlike any I'd ever heard echoed from the night forest. I was shocked by the heat. Nighttime should have cooled things down, but the heat stuck to me, the air heavy and wet. Ramon had said that's probably why the Defender was imprisoned in the Caribbean, the heat sapping his power.

"Is it OK to talk?" I whispered.

"Softly, m'lady," Mr. Winters answered. "I think we're alone, but you never know."

I had been wondering about something since my arrival at the North Pole. "Are there other kids like me being trained as Defenders?"

"Well, there's no one quite like you, m'lady." Mr. Winters smiled. "But, yes, we have other trainees."

"Where are they? Why aren't they at the North Pole?"

"School, of course. Defenders have normal lives, too, and families. Your father lived in New York with you and your mother, as I recall."

I nodded. "So when do you train them?"

"Summer mostly. Sometimes school breaks."

My eyes lit up and I asked excitedly, "So over Christmas they'll come?" The idea of meeting other kids just like me—ones who wouldn't mock a girl just for loving Christmas—was thrilling.

"No, m'lady," Mr. Winters said. "Christmas is when we're busiest. No time for training." I slumped in disappointment. "You'll meet them eventually," Mr. Winters added.

I nodded dejectedly. "Where does our power come from?"

"No one really knows. But I look at it this way. Where did Beethoven's musical ability come from, or Amelia Earhart's fearlessness, or Martin Luther King, Jr.'s wisdom? All from the same mysterious place. All humans have something special inside. This power is what we have."

I felt better after hearing that. Mr. Winters had the knack good teachers possess of making something complicated easier to understand. For the first time, I felt like maybe it was OK to have this power and that I was where I was supposed to be, with other kids like me (eventually), with people who might even become like family. And maybe, just maybe, I'd get a part of my real family back. I prayed that my father was the one who had called out to me, that he was deep within that mountain and he'd emerge from the forest with the rest of the Defenders, miraculously walking back into my life.

It had been only about forty-five minutes, but it seemed like hours. The strange sounds of the forest and the occasional sigh from Mr. Winters were the only things that broke the silence.

"How long do you think they'll be?" I whispered.

"And how would I know that?" Mr. Winters snapped,

with an edge to his voice that cut straight to my heart. I felt stupid. Mr. Winters had never once been impatient with me. He must have realized how he sounded, and his tone softened. "I'm sorry, dear heart. I feel as helpless as you. But they can handle themselves."

"OK," I said, trying not to let him hear the shakiness in my voice. We sat quietly, watching and waiting. The reindeer munched endlessly on the forest grass. I hopped off the sleigh to pet one of the deer, but he seemed uninterested, continuing to eat as if I weren't even there. I petted him anyway, because it made me feel better, our magical connection calming my nerves.

Suddenly there was a rumble from the mountain. Mr. Winters leaped from the sleigh and landed beside me, staring at the forest into which Santa and the Defenders had disappeared. His body seemed to twitch. "Wait here," he said, and before I could object, Mr. Winters took off into the forest. I stood there, alone, just me and the reindeer. I listened closely, hoping for any clues that might tell me what was happening. Another rumble came from the mountain. Then another. Then a long silence. Even the reindeer had stopped munching. Did they know their riders might be in danger? They suddenly stood taller and made weird snorting sounds. They heard something.

What that something was came crashing through the trees. The Defenders, led by Santa and Mr. Winters, charged out of the forest. Two Defenders carried a man, his face covered by shadow and impossibly long hair. They struggled with him and glanced behind as if checking for anyone who might have followed. Trailing them was Ramon. He was limping badly.

"To the sky," Santa yelled, and the Defenders ran to their mounts. I started to do the same but realized I had no idea which was mine. Mr. Winters grabbed me roughly by the arm and pulled me to my deer, lifting me on.

"What's happening?" I asked. Nothing had emerged from the forest to chase us. "What are we running from?"

"The Defenders collapsed the tunnel so he couldn't follow. But we fear he'll circle back around."

"Who?"

"We don't know," Mr. Winters said, jumping onto his deer. "And we're not sticking around to find out."

"Why don't the Defenders fight him?"

"He's powerful. Santa senses it. For now, we fly. Go, Carol!" Mr. Winters spurred on his reindeer, and off he went. I did the same, glancing back to see Ramon, clearly in pain, climbing gingerly onto the back of his mount. He was the last to take off, and he trailed behind. I pulled on my reins to slow down.

"Hurry, Ramon!" I yelled. I could see nothing—no one chasing us, no apparent danger. But suddenly, I felt a presence, a powerful force, like a shift in the atmosphere when a violent storm is looming. Panic bubbled inside me.

"I'm coming, *mi'ja*. Fly!" Then came the sound. A roar of an engine. Then what sounded like the sonic boom of a jet breaking the sound barrier. My ears popped. The air felt soupy, as if we were trying to fly through water. From the mountain below, circling from the front entrance to the cave, flew a tiny figure. Not on a reindeer, but on a flying machine that trailed white smoke and resembled a tricked-out jet engine with wings. The figure appeared to be a man, and as he drew closer, I could see a mask that looked like a weird mix of what hockey goalies and welders wear, the eyes glowing. He held what appeared to be a long stick, some kind of staff, which glowed green on each end. He was gaining on us. Five hundred yards away. Four hundred yards. Three hundred.

Ramon was still at the rear and glanced back. I saw him veer off. He turned to face our pursuer. The Masked Man slowed his machine down, measuring his foe. I yelled, "No!" and watched as Ramon threw his right hand toward the Masked Man as if hurling a thunderbolt. The air between them rippled, and the Masked Man held up his staff to block the attack. He was knocked sideways on his machine. But it stopped him for only a moment. He gathered himself, and the machine hovered and sputtered. Ramon turned to us and yelled, "Go!"

Mr. Winters grabbed the reins of my deer, pulling me away. "Now, dear heart!"

I heard real fear in his voice. I shivered, even in the heat. "We can't leave him!" I shouted.

"Santa must be protected at all costs," Mr. Winters said, and he took off at full speed toward the others, dragging my reindeer with him. I glanced back at Ramon and watched him watching us. He gave me a little salute, and then smiled his brilliant, white smile, visible even in the moonlight. He turned and spurred his reindeer toward the Masked Man. The enemy pulled back his staff and hurled whatever terrible power he possessed at my new friend. The air shimmered. There was another sonic boom. Ramon and his reindeer were blasted backward. Ramon tumbled from the back of his mount. He and the deer seemed to hang in midair, as if a residue of Defender magic protected them for one final moment. Then they fell, straight down to the forest of Ramon's homeland, to the mountains he had roamed as a child. I screamed, "Noooo!" The Masked Man's head snapped around, and he gazed directly at me, the eyes of his mask glowing green like his staff. He rocketed toward us, ready to attack.

Then he was gone. The hot, muggy air was now cold and crisp. The tears on my cheeks turned chill in the night air. We had made the leap out of the Dominican Republic. I knew we were back at the North Pole. We had escaped. Ramon had sacrificed himself to save us.

CHAPTER 8

Reunion

We flew in silence through the bitter North Pole sky, and I cried softly, hoping no one would hear. But Mr. Winters slowed beside me and put a hand on my shoulder. "I'm so sorry, dear heart."

"We shouldn't . . . have left him," I said, trying to catch my breath between sobs.

"It could not be helped. Ramon understood."

"I don't," I said, angrily snapping my legs against the sides of my reindeer, which bolted ahead. I had to get away from Mr. Winters, from all of them. He didn't follow me. But Santa did. He and the long-haired man I'd caught just a glimpse of were in the sleigh. I was so sad and angry that I'd almost forgotten the Defender Ramon had given himself up to save. Santa guided his sleigh next to me, and I wiped away my tears as best I could. The man sat up and studied me. His hair hung well past his waist, covering his legs like a blanket. The customary streak of white twisted wildly through the red. There was something familiar about him. A tear trickled down his cheek and into his beard, freezing in the arctic air. Before he said a single word, I knew. "Carol?" he asked, with eyes wide.

"Daddy?" I responded. When he nodded, I launched myself from the back of my reindeer and onto the sleigh, throwing my arms around him. He rocked me back and forth, stroking my hair, kissing my head again and again, and muttering, "Oh, thank God. Thank God. My baby."

"Why did you leave me?" I asked, sobbing.

"Oh, sweetheart. I didn't mean to."

I buried my face in his hair. His clothes were a tattered mess. He smelled like sweat and a musty basement. His beard was ragged and tangled. He wore no coat, but the hair was so thick and long he probably didn't need one. He stroked my forehead. His skin was rough, but I didn't mind. I felt a surge of joy and squeezed him hard around the waist. Then I remembered Ramon and felt guilty for my happiness. I thought of Ramon's family and the love and warmth in his home. I knew that he would want this for me, to be able to hug my dad for the first time since I was five years old. But now his family, his poor *abuela*, they could no longer hug him.

The sleigh bumped down and slowed to a stop. We were back at Santa's, and Mrs. Claus came running out. Nori and Gerta helped me down from the sleigh and then reached for Dad. He waved them away. "My strength returns." He stood up straight, breathed the cold air deeply, and hopped off the sleigh. He stumbled a bit, swaying as if trying to stay upright on a skateboard, but quickly regained his balance and put his arm around me. He walked barefoot through the snow. Mrs. Claus threw her arms around the both of us. "Welcome home," she said. An awful silence settled like a fog over the group. Mrs. Claus looked at Santa, who hung his head. "Who, dear?" she whispered.

"Ramon," he said quietly, and Mrs. Claus cried and embraced her husband. My insides churned like the sea on a rocky shore. Sadness, joy, fear, relief—they all crashed against each other. There were too many emotions that day. Was this what it meant to be a Defender? If that was the case, maybe I wasn't up to the task. Maybe I didn't belong.

Dad was like a different person when he emerged from the bathroom. His face was smooth and shaven, glowing pink. He definitely resembled his younger brother, but his features were softer, kinder. Less like chiseled granite, more like sculpted clay. He had freckles just like mine, though lighter and not as many, and his eyes were also green. He looked remarkably young, the life and energy returning to him. I wasn't even sure how old he was.

Dad carried a plastic bag full of the hair that once hung to his knees. "You don't mind keeping this for me, do you, Carol?" he asked, looking serious. It occurred to me that I didn't know my father at all. I knew only fuzzy memories and what I imagined him to be. I remembered playing with him in the snow and drinking hot chocolate and seeing his face light up when I opened the carved wooden Santa. That was it. Was he funny or serious? Did he get mad easily or have the patience of Mr. Winters? Was he a happy person or moody? I took too long to respond, and he laughed. "I'm joking, Angel Butt," he said, and hearing those words made me feel like I was five again. I started to cry. "What's wrong, honey?" Dad asked, pulling me close. He no longer smelled of sweat and mustiness. He had a cinnamon scent that sweetened the air.

"I missed you. I miss Ramon. I miss Mom."

"I know, sweetie. So do I. But I'm back now, and we're together. We have to laugh again. We have to be happy. Your mom would want that, and so would Ramon."

"OK," I said. Then something occurred to me. "How did you know Mom died?"

"My captors told me," he said and then paused, as if trying not to cry himself.

"Who kidnapped you?"

"I don't know who the big guy is, but there were two former Defenders involved. When I asked them to explain themselves, they refused to talk, saying only that they were tired of wasting their gift." He touched my lock of white hair, studying it. "So, Santa says you have it, too." I nodded. "And he says my brother took you in. I'll bet that was a barrel of laughs." He winked. "Tell me everything. I want to hear all about it."

I nodded again and then went into probably way too much detail about my uncle's toy company and how rich he was; about Broward Academy and how hard school could be and how I felt like an outcast; about Amelia and how she was my closest, most loyal friend, and how she was separated from her father just like I was; about Vincent Cato and the other kids and how they called me Christmas Carol; about the old reindeer that flew and wreaked havoc at the festival; about how Mr. Winters showed up and was so weird and so cool; about the trip to New York and meeting Santa and then stopping time and saving the little boy. Dad listened and laughed, not once interrupting. He never stopped smiling, and I didn't feel silly at all, even though I knew I was being a silly little kid, rambling on and on. I talked about how Uncle Christopher took care of me and gave me everything I could ever want but never hugged me and rarely smiled and worked all the time.

The smile finally disappeared from Dad's face. "My brother and I are night and day. Mom used to call us Cain and Abel after the biblical brothers. A bit harsh, I think, since Cain did in his poor brother, but she made her point." Dad put his head down, lost in thought. "Chris was always jealous of me. When I turned fourteen and started leaving in the summers to train as a Defender, I had to keep it a secret, of course, and make up a story about a special camp I got to attend. He barely talked to me after that. I think he felt abandoned every summer when we could have been doing fun things together."

"I feel sorry for him," I blurted out. I hadn't really thought much about it before, but I realized it was the truth. There was something sad about my uncle. "He seems lonely."

Dad stroked my hair and tears glistened in his eyes. "You have a kind heart, Carol. My brother chooses to be the way he is, I think. That company is all he's ever cared about, and he steamrolls anyone who gets in his way. Regardless, I owe him a debt of gratitude for taking you in. Maybe we can patch things up."

I nodded, not sure what else to say. I wondered if my uncle missed me and if he was searching for me. Surely the authorities were hunting for Mr. Winters; everybody probably assumed he was some twisted sicko who had wormed his way into Broward and kidnapped me. I thought of Amelia and how much she must miss me— just as much as I missed her. I wondered if Dad and I would go to Hillsboro at some point. Florida had never been his home. Syracuse was. "What do we do now?" I asked. "Where do we go?"

"I don't know," Dad said. "I haven't had time to think about it."

"You will stay here, of course." Mrs. Claus floated into the room. I hadn't even heard her approach. She was like a cat. "You will rest and recover."

Santa appeared. He seemed to go wherever Mrs. Claus went. "Christmas approaches," Santa said, looking at my father. "I hesitate to even ask, but I need all of my Defenders. You weren't the only one who vanished. And with Ramon's loss . . ."

"What do you mean?" I asked, feeling a stab in my heart at the mention of our lost friend's name. "He can't go back to being a Defender, not after all he's been through." Santa looked almost ashamed as he turned away. Mrs. Claus touched me gently on the shoulder.

"Carol, honey, I made a pledge," Dad said.

"I don't care about your stupid pledge!" I shouted. "I can't lose you again. I won't!"

"Carol!" Dad said, his tone firm. "I'm sorry, honey, but that is not your decision. I chose what to do with my life. I have a gift, and it must not be wasted."

My face turned fiery red. I wanted to scream. I wanted to stomp out of the room. But then I thought of something, and a calm settled over me. I smiled, and my father studied me. I could tell he was puzzled. He didn't really know me either. "Then I'm going with you," I said.

"Absolutely not."

"I have a gift," I said with a smirk. "And it must not be wasted." I knew I was being a brat, but I enjoyed turning those words around on him.

"You're too young. Christmas is too close."

"You can teach me."

"No!"

"So it's OK for you to risk your life but not me?"

"Yes."

"That's not fair," I said, folding my arms across my chest and puffing out my bottom lip.

Santa interrupted. "She understands the elves, Brian," he said softly.

My father whipped his head around to look at Santa. "What? None of us can."

"They call her the Gifted One."

"That can't be," Dad said.

"It is," Mrs. Claus replied. "I understand your fears, but she has great power. Who better to teach her to use it than her father?"

Dad thought about this. We watched him expectantly. I uncrossed my arms and glared at him, mad at myself for being mad at him so soon after his return, but unable to control how I felt. When his eyes met mine, however, the anger just vanished. He smiled and reached out to stroke my hair. "You're so young, Carol."

"I'm almost thirteen, Daddy."

"You are, aren't you? I've missed so much. And you lost out on having a father."

"You're here now," I said. "Teach me."

My father looked at Santa and Mrs. Claus and then back to me. He sighed and slowly nodded.

We probably should have practiced farther from Santa's. Dad and I stood in the front yard, between the house and the reindeer barn, while Mr. Winters watched from the front porch. "Just curious, m'lady. Want to see the Gifted One in action." He winked. I wished people would quit calling me that. Talk about pressure! What if the elves were wrong? Maybe I was just good with the elf language or something. Sort of like Amelia. She spoke Spanish and English, of course, and when we took French, it came naturally to her, while my tongue tripped all over itself every time I tried to roll an "r." She sounded like she was from Paris. I sounded like a cat coughing up a hair ball.

Dad stood beside me in the trampled-down snow. It was late evening, the lights of the decorated tree in front of the house sparkling in the near night. I had on a heavy winter coat, gloves, hat, the works—all provided by Mrs. Claus—but Dad wore a light jacket, no gloves, no hat. "You don't know how good this feels, Angel Butt," he said, spreading his arms and tilting his head back. "I was miserable in that hot cell for so long." I understood a little of what he felt. Despite Mrs. Claus's insistence that I bundle up, I was swelteringly hot. How did I ever stand Florida? I slipped off my gloves, glancing at the house to make sure Mrs. Claus wasn't watching. I tossed the gloves into the snow and waited for my father to finish his whole embrace-the-cold thing. He smiled broadly and waved his arms toward his face as if gathering smells from a freshly-baked pie, then he spun around and around. Good gravy, I was from a weird family.

"So what do you know so far?" he asked at last. "You slowed down time to save that boy, right? How did you do that?"

"I don't remember. It just happened." I nodded over to Mr. Winters. "He gave me lessons in the freezer at school."

Dad raised an eyebrow. "My daughter getting time-bending lessons in a meat locker." He laughed and leaned in close. "That Mr. Winters is an odd one, with the whole 'm'lady' bit." This from a man who called me Angel Butt and spun in circles soaking in the cold. "The first thing I learned was how to create what we call an NP, a North Pulse. It's like a burst of energy. Watch." He circled his hand slowly and closed it to a fist, then flung his hand open in the direction of the mailbox at the front fence. The mailbox rattled, and the red lever fell with a clank.

"Cool," I said.

"Yeah, it is kinda cool."

"How do you do it?"

"Think of space and time as sort of a web we don't see."

"Yeah, Mr. Winters explained that."

Dad nodded. "The gift we have is being able to do things with that web. You just have to trust it's there." I looked around, as if I might be able to see what he was talking about, but all I saw was the house, the Christmas tree, the mailbox, the reindeer barn, and endless snow. "Concentrate on seeing what's not visible, and then move your hand through it, circling like you're gathering up the web in a ball. Then just throw it. The tighter the circle, the smaller the ball. How hard you concentrate factors in, as does the length of the buildup. It all determines the strength and size of the pulse. It's not an exact science. Your emotions affect it, so you have to stay on an even keel to control it. Understand?"

"I think so."

"OK, give it a try." He pointed to the Christmas tree. "See that red ribbon on the lower branch? Try and move it with an NP." He stepped closer and took my right hand in his, mimicking the motion his own hand had made. "Concentrate on the air around us."

I nodded, and he stepped back. I closed my eyes and concentrated, trying to picture the web. How in the world do you see something that's invisible? I circled my hand and closed my fingers as if grabbing a handful of strands. Then I threw my arm toward the ribbon. Nothing. The ribbon didn't even flutter.

"That's OK," my father said. "No one gets it the first day. Try again." I wound up, grabbed the web, and then flung it toward the tree. Nothing. I tried again. Then again. Then again, getting more and more frustrated.

Suddenly, a thought occurred to me. Duh. I switched hands. I concentrated so hard I thought my head might burst. I circled my hand again and again, increasing the speed. I closed my hand on the invisible web, imagining that I was grabbing a huge handful of strands, making a giant ball. Then with all my might, I flung my left hand toward the ribbon. The air pulsed violently. My father jumped back as if getting out of the way of a speeding bus. Mr. Winters ducked his head into his arms and threw himself to the porch floor. The ribbon blew off the tree. I heard a violent cracking sound. Tree branches snapped. The bulbs on the string of lights burst. The tree swayed, and then started to fall. "Oh, no," Dad muttered. Mr. Winters glanced up from the porch floor, scrambling away just in time. The upper branches caught in the power lines and yanked them down. Across the yard, the generator they were attached to exploded in a shower of sparks. The tree fell as if in slow motion onto the roof of the porch. The top branches, wires and all, crashed through a window on the second floor of Santa's house. The porch roof caved in. Another generator in the distance blew. Everything went dark. Then there was silence.

Mr. Winters was picking himself up out of the snow. I looked at my father, whose mouth hung open, his eyes wide. I wondered if I was in trouble. He looked at me. "So you're left-handed," he said. "Good to know, Angel Butt." Then he smiled.

CHAPTER 9

Visiting the Elves

The elves made the repairs within a day, and it was as if nothing had happened, as if I hadn't almost destroyed Santa's house. I watched from the front window as they worked. Dozens of elves scurried around, chattering telepathically at such speed I couldn't understand much of what was being said, though I did overhear *Gifted One* and wondered what they were saying about me. Maybe they were cursing me for all of the unexpected work less than two weeks before Christmas. Do elves have their own swear words?

The last one stayed just past nightfall, touching up the paint on the beams they had put in to reinforce the repaired porch roof. I watched him work and then wondered if *he* was even a *him*. The elves were beautiful, not at all like the stout, little creatures who appeared in every Christmas movie and cartoon ever made. They were lean and pale and athletic.

The elf snapped the lid on his paint can shut and cleaned his brush in a small bucket. I could hear him humming softly in my mind—so freaky!—and he glanced at me through the window and smiled. Had he heard my thoughts? Embarrassed, I retreated into the shadows of Santa's house to look for my father and the others, who, last I checked, were gathered around the dining room table discussing plans for Christmas. "We're always look-ing for ways to make the night run smoother," Mr. Winters told me. I nodded, not the least bit interested when he started talking about "efficiency" and "distribution" and "volume," stuff that sounded suspiciously like math. I pre-ferred to watch the elves.

As I walked, I heard a soft voice inside my head: *Come, my child.* I turned quickly. No one was there. But a shadow passed the window. I checked to see if anyone was watch-ing and then slipped out the door. The elf was already across the yard. *Follow me, Gifted One.* The elf never glanced back as he glided past the reindeer barn and into an open field lit only by the full moon. His feet skimmed across the snow, not leaving a mark, while mine sank with each grueling step. I loved the snow, but that still didn't make it any easier to walk in when it was two feet deep. The elf stopped occasionally to wait for me, still not looking back. I wondered if he could read my mind, and I concentrated hard, directing the question toward him. *Can you hear my thoughts?*

Only if you want me to, or if you do not guard them.

How do I do that?

You just do.

I nodded and followed the elf into a thick forest. The trees blocked out the moon, and in the sudden darkness, it was clear that the elf glowed, a pale white, as if the moon's rays clung to him. The elf lit the way through the trees. *How long have you lived here?* I asked.

Centuries by your measure of time.

You live for centuries?

Yes.

So cool! We emerged into a huge clearing, the bright moon making it seem like day after being in the dark forest.

I gasped. In the center of the clearing was the largest tree I had ever seen, as large as a redwood, but more twisty, like an oak or a chestnut, its branches extending every which way, curling outward and upward and sideward. And weaving in and around every branch was ice! But not like ice any human has ever seen. A blue, glowing sort of ice that formed steps and slides and houses and tables and benches and chairs. An entire frozen world. There were ice sculptures everywhere, of Santa, reindeer, elves, Christmas trees, toys, and giant presents with intricately tied bows. The elves glided down slides like snowboarders on a mountain. They hurried up and down steps, as if they were flying. They sat on benches, chatting away, lips not moving, making no sound. The tree world was alive with activity, but strangely silent.

Hurry, my child. The voice in my head made me jump, and I let out a little squeal, which echoed through the ice world. A hundred heads turned. *The Gifted One . . . He brought her . . . She has come . . . So beautiful.*

Beautiful? I liked the sound of that, but I still wasn't crazy about the whole "gifted" thing. *Where are we going?*

She wants to see you.

Who?

The Ancient One.

Boy, they really liked titles in this place. Gifted One. Ancient One. I wondered if there was a Stupid One or an Annoying One. Maybe a Gassy One. The elf glanced at me. Oops, I needed to be more careful guarding my thoughts. *Why does she want to see me?*

No one knows why she does anything. She's . . . the elf hesitated *. . . unique.*

Unique? What did that mean?

You shall see.

We reached what appeared to be the edge of the kingdom, and I realized that the giant tree, the clearing, it was surrounded by forest. A huge circle. Along the far edge of the forest sat a small wooden house, nothing like the ice structures in which the rest of the elves lived. A plume of white smoke curled from the chimney. The elf stopped on the front porch and put his hand up to knock. But before he could, the door slowly swung open, creaking like the place was haunted. He jumped back, startled, and I peered in. It was a log cabin—one large room—and in the corner was a bed covered by an antique-looking quilt. A table with three chairs sat next to what looked like some sort of icebox. *Welcome, my sweet,* came a voice in my head. The elf and I stepped into the house. A couch and chair sat in front of a fire that crackled in the hearth. What kind of North Pole elf would need a fire?

The voice returned. *A remnant of my life among your kind.* I searched for the source of the voice. From the shadows stepped a female, stooped over, her long, white hair hanging nearly to the floor. She was beautiful like the other elves, but wrinkled around her eyes and mouth, the blue ice of her eyes dulled by time. Her hands were gnarled, and she moved slowly, without the effortless grace of the others. She wore a flowing blue robe tied loosely at the waist. This, without a doubt, was the Ancient One. If elves lived for centuries, then she must have been several hundred years old. She motioned for me to join her at the table. My guide stood near the door, fidgeting, eyes darting around nervously.

The Ancient One sat across from me, groaning as she lowered herself into the chair. She let out a long sigh once she was seated. *How old are you?* I asked, only half intentionally, thinking the thought but not sure I should actually share it.

The Ancient One laughed. "Don't you know it's not polite to ask someone's age?"

"I'm sorry," I said, then realized she'd spoken aloud. "Hey, you can talk!"

"Of course I can. How else could I have lived among your kind?"

"Oh, yeah."

"As for my age," she continued, "by your standards, I'm more than 500 years old."

"Holy moly, that's old!"

"Indeed," the elf said. "And I feel every year in my bones."

"What did you mean about living among my kind?"

"Just that. I left this place a long, long time ago."

"And you lived with humans?"

"Yes."

"Why?"

"Restlessness, curiosity, stubbornness, arrogance. I was not an easy elf when I was young."

"Where did you live? And who with? What is your name? Why did you want to see me?"

"So many questions, my sweet." She chuckled softly.

"They call me Noelle, and I shall tell you anything you want to know. But my tale is too long to tell in just one sitting. There is, however, another way." She leaned across the table toward me. Her eyes came alive, the dullness of age burned away like morning fog on a sunny day. "If you're willing."

"Sure, I guess," I said hesitantly.

"It's called The Sharing, and it's a bit overwhelming. You might even feel ill afterward. But I think you'll learn something that will surprise you."

I nodded nervously. "Let's do it. I can take it."

"A girl after my own heart," the elf said, smiling. The Ancient One turned to the elf guide. *Be gone*, she snapped. *I'll summon you when I'm done.* He turned and sprinted out the door, slamming it behind him. "Annoying things, other elves can be," the Ancient One mumbled. "So afraid of anything outside their little bubble. All they want to do is watch the world."

"What do you mean?" I asked.

"Yes, yes, I suppose I should explain. The Sharing can wait." The Ancient One closed her eyes, raised her hands above her head, and then moved them in opposite directions, in a circular motion, bringing them together at her waist to complete a circle. The air shimmered, like heat on a desert highway, and suddenly there was a picture, slowly coming into focus. I was looking at Santa, my father, Mr. Winters, and the other Defenders gathered around the table. They were talking, but I couldn't hear them. Santa glanced up, nodded toward us, and turned back to the discussion. Mr. Winters noticed and looked in the same direction. But his eyes couldn't fix on anything. He couldn't see us! "This is a portal," the Ancient One explained. "You see them clearly, yes?"

"Like I'm looking through a window."

"Remarkable," she said quietly. "The fact that you can see tells us you're special. Besides you, only Santa can."

"But what do you use it for?"

"Many things. Have you ever wondered how Santa fits all the toys for all the world's children into his sleigh?"

"Yes! All kids wonder that."

"He doesn't. Elves deliver a constant stream of toys through a portal all the way through Christmas morning. The Defenders slow time, and we provide the toys."

"Awesome!"

"We elves also can travel through a portal to anywhere we choose. But we're only supposed to watch, not travel, not meddle in human affairs." She waved her hand, and the portal disappeared. "But I wanted more. I wanted to really see what we were watching. So I left."

"You ran away?"

"You can see for yourself in The Sharing." The Ancient One moved her chair close, facing me, our knees touching. "Are you ready, my child?" I nodded solemnly. She put out her hands, palms up. I placed my hands in hers. The skin was cool but rough with time and wear. "Close your eyes," she ordered. My body trembled. I braced for the unknown. The elf's hands suddenly clamped on mine so hard I gasped in pain. I tried to pull away, but she held them tighter and tighter. I thought she might crush the bones in my fingers. How could she be so strong? Before I could tell her she was hurting me, there was a flash of light. My eyes were still closed, so it must have been in my mind.

Then a picture formed of a young female elf, tall and beautiful and full of life. It was the Ancient One, a long, long time ago. I watched her leave the elf kingdom and explore the world, country after country, city after city, for years and years. I watched her live among humans, work among them, pass herself off as one of them. And though she knew it was foolish, I saw her fall in love with a handsome man. And I watched her marry that man and have two daughters, the girls living long lives, thanks to their elf blood.

But eventually, as they grew old and she didn't, the elf had to return to her world. She built herself a house on the edge of the ice kingdom and re-created a home like the one she'd had with her husband and daughters. Through the portals she watched her grandchildren, then her great-grandchildren, and her great-great-grandchildren, and on and on, until at last she saw a little girl with red hair, and a father and a mother who were special and powerful and filled with love they showered on their precious child.

I saw the father and the young girl playing in the snow, and then I heard the voice of the mother calling from inside. That's when I realized I was watching myself! My mother appeared at the front door, hands on her hips, looking delicate and beautiful. "Come inside, Carol!" she yelled. I could see it now, the pale skin that almost glowed, a slight point to her ears, blue eyes of ice, and hair that was blond but looked almost radiant white when the light hit it. She was the spitting image of a young Noelle. My mother was part elf. I was part elf!

And then I awoke, sprawled on the couch, my head lying in the lap of the Ancient One, who stroked my hair and looked down at me, tears in her eyes. I smiled at her. "So you're my great-great-great-something-grand-mother?"

She wiped away the tears and kissed my forehead. "I am indeed, my sweet."

"Does Dad know?"

She nodded to the chair next to the fire. My father sat watching us, and tears filled his eyes, too. "I do now," he said.

"I sent for your father once we were done with The Sharing. You were out for a good while. How do you feel?"

"Hungry." I realized I was starving. Light streamed through the windows. I had been there all night!

"My, my, you are a strong one." The old elf helped me up. I was woozy and had to grab the arm of the couch to steady myself. The Ancient One and I made our way to the table, which was filled with bacon and eggs and sausage and biscuits. The elf spooned huge helpings of everything onto my plate and poured me a tall glass of milk. She looked at my father, then at me, and smiled. Once again, tears gathered in her ancient blue eyes.

"It's truly a miracle," she said. "I'm sharing a meal with my family. I never thought I'd live to see the day. Now eat!"

"Thank you . . ." I hesitated, not sure what to call the Ancient One. Yes, she was my grandmother, sort of, but so far removed that it seemed strange to call her that. But I could think of nothing else, and she was family, so I said, "Thank you . . . Grandmother." My father smiled, and the Ancient One's eyes lit up and I knew I'd made the right choice. Grandmother hugged me tightly.

CHAPTER 10

The Cane Muting

"Why didn't you try to meet us?" I asked. "Your grand-children, I mean. Me."

Grandmother and I sat on her front porch watching the elves scurry around the ice kingdom, shuttling back and forth to the toy factory for the last-minute Christmas push. I'd been visiting her every evening after spending the week training with Dad, hanging out in Santa's house being spoiled by Mrs. Claus, and visiting the toy factory—which, I have to say, was awesome! There were toys as far as the eye could see, elves hammering and drilling and glu-ing and whatever else you need to do to make toys, which were added to the ones Santa bought from his suppliers. But as awesome as it was to see all of that, I most enjoyed my time with the Ancient One. Having a grandmother was a new experience for me, a wonderful experience. As sad as it made me to think about it, I now understood better how much Ramon's *abuela* meant to him.

Grandmother talked of her life and told me stories about the man she married, my great-great-great-whatever-grandfather. She still missed him. "Think about how you miss your mother," she said. "And how you missed your father. Now multiply that by one hundred, losing grandchild after grandchild after grandchild. It would have been more than I could bear. That's why I stayed away."

"But won't you lose me?"

She gave me a sad smile. "You are wise for your years, Carol. Yes, there's always that chance. But I am very old. Even elves die. I suspect I may be gone before you."

"But then *I* will be losing *you*!"

"That's the way of the world, I'm afraid. We all suffer loss. It's how well we love those in our lives while they're around that matters."

We talked for hours, Grandmother asking about school, about Mr. Winters, about my powers, about

Amelia, who she said "sounds wonderful. Always treasure a friend." And, naturally, she asked about my uncle. She frowned whenever I spoke of him and his behavior. But I tried to paint a rosier picture. After all, he wasn't obligated to take care of me, but he had. He was my blood, and I loved him.

The day she asked about him, it occurred to me that it was the Friday before I normally would be leaving school for Christmas vacation, a day my uncle, not Gus, would have come to get me. I wondered if Uncle Christopher missed picking me up from school every Friday. Maybe he secretly cherished those moments we spent together, but he just wasn't good at showing his emotions, his chiseled exterior hiding a tender heart. I wanted to believe that.

"Can we see what he's doing?" I asked. "Can you make a portal?"

"They are not to be created lightly," Grandmother said. "And, anyway, I suspect you are perfectly capable of making one yourself. When I showed you my memories, the elf abilities—if you didn't already possess them—were passed to you."

"Holy moly! You mean I can see anything? Anywhere?"

"Yes, you can also focus on someone you know and a portal will open to wherever they are."

"So cool!"

"You may try it, but you must not abuse the privilege."

"How do I do it?"

"Just focus as hard as you can on what you want to see and make a circle with your hands, like this." She demonstrated.

I nodded and closed my eyes, bringing up an image of my uncle hunched over his desk, as I'd seen him countless times. I concentrated all my energies on his existence. I kept my eyes closed, my hands straight up above my head, making a large circle by extending them outward. I grasped the web of time and space. I felt a ripple in the air. I opened my eyes and caught a glimpse of my uncle. The image was shaky but then crystallized. He was at his factory, sitting at his desk, leaning back in his chair and holding the polished black rock with the International Toy logo engraved on it, rubbing the stone absentmindedly. Suddenly, he turned as if someone had called his name, and then the image collapsed. I'd lost it.

"That was curious," Grandmother said.

"What?"

"The way the portal dissolved. I've never seen that happen."

"Maybe I lost concentration," I suggested. "Or maybe it's because I'm mostly human."

"Perhaps." She said nothing more, adrift in thought.

"Can I try my school?"

"Yes, but this is the last one for now."

"OK." I repeated the procedure, concentrating on the classroom in which I'd spent so many hours, concentrating on my best friend. The portal was strong this time and the image clear. Amelia, Vincent Cato, and my other classmates stared glumly at a teacher I recognized as Old Mole Nose. No wonder everyone looked miserable. My chair was unoccupied, but a large red-and-green ribbon with a photograph of me in the center hung from the seat back. On my desk sat a single candy cane and a placard that read in big red letters, WE MISS YOU, CHRISTMAS CAROL. All the kids had signed it—even Vincent! Next to Amelia's signature she had written the sweet English phrase her father put at the end of his letters to her: "I will love you much eternity. Hugs and kisses and butterfly wishes." Amelia looked at the empty chair and sighed. She turned away like she might cry. My eyes welled up. I felt awful not being able to tell her I was safe and happy, as happy as I'd ever been. I wanted to tell her that Santa Claus was real and wonderful, and the elves were magical and kind, and weird Mr. Winters was so much more than we ever imagined. But the image dissolved. I wiped away tears.

"That's enough for now, dear," Grandmother said quietly.

I nodded. It certainly was.

"Tell me about the Masked Man," Grandmother said. It was the day before Christmas Eve, and Santa's house and the elves' ice kingdom were in a frenzy. But I could do nothing. I wasn't allowed to go with the Defenders. I knew zilch about making toys. I had no clue about planning or toy distribution or how to best travel the world in a single night. Basically, I was just in everyone's way. So I figured I may as well hang out with someone else who also seemed to be forgotten. ("The Ancient One and the Gifted One are the Useless Ones," Grandmother joked.)

"I don't like to think about him," I answered.

"I know, my sweet, but I want to learn about his power, and who knows which one of us might be called upon to fight him. I have this terrible feeling he's planning something."

I trembled at the thought. "He flew some kind of machine. And he held a long stick."

"A staff, you mean?"

"I guess. Like a wizard. He aimed it at Ramon and knocked him out of the sky."

"I suspect this Masked Man was once a Defender, or has similar powers," Grandmother said. "And I believe he discovered something I thought only elves knew. Even most of them are unaware of it."

"What?"

Grandmother leaned in close. "I suspect his staff is made from the wood of the giant fir trees in the Crystal Forest, which is in a remote part of the North Pole. That was the home of a race of elves long gone from this earth. But the forest remains, and the trees hold remnants of their ancient magic."

"But how would he know that?"

"There have been others like me, elves who wandered off to explore the world. Some never returned. Perhaps the Masked Man met one, and the elf shared the secret."

"But what does the rod do?"

"It's an amplifier. For one with power, it concentrates that power and magnifies it tenfold." The thought made me shudder. Imagine a Defender's power times ten. No wonder Ramon stood no chance. No wonder Santa and Mr. Winters made us flee that awful day. "And because the staff is elfin in nature," Grandmother continued, "he would be able to make portals or do anything elves can."

She stood up slowly from the chair next to the fire, her bones creaking. She crossed the room to a closed door I'd never seen her open. She pulled a skeleton key from a pocket in her robe and turned the lock. The door swung open, its hinges groaning. She reached into the dark closet and removed a burlap sack, which was tied shut with twine. She returned slowly to her chair and sat down, breathing hard.

"What is that?" I asked.

"A way to fight back," she answered and pulled out what looked like a giant candy cane. It was about three feet long, curved at the end just like a walking cane, but painted with red and white stripes. She rapped her knuckles lightly on the cane, which was about as thick as the handle of a baseball bat.

"Wood?" I asked.

"Made from a fir tree in the Crystal Forest, which I explored when I left the North Pole. I carved it into this shape to keep it hidden. No one would question a wooden cane. I kept it with me through my travels."

"But why did you paint it like a candy cane?"

Grandmother laughed. "I'm a smart aleck, I suppose. I did that when I returned here. You have noticed I live at the North Pole, right? Where it always seems to be Christmas?" She laughed again. "Looks like just another holiday decoration. It also allows me to more easily give it to you. If I handed you a weapon, what would your father say? Or Santa?"

"That I couldn't have it. That I'm not ready."

"Exactly. But if the crazy, old elf lady gave a wooden candy cane to the girl who loves Christmas, no one would think twice about it." She grinned, mischief dancing in her eyes.

I smiled as she passed me the cane. When it touched my hand, I swear I felt the wood pulse, as if it were a living organism and I could feel its heartbeat. There was even a hum, like electricity, though I wondered if that was just in my mind, the power coursing through me. "How does it work?" I asked, turning it over in my hands. The cane was as smooth as Santa's polished hardwood floors.

"Your father's teaching you to focus your powers, correct?" Grandmother asked. I nodded. "Just hold the cane in front of you as you do, and it will collect the power. Then thrust the cane in the direction you want to release that power, like one of those pulses you destroyed Santa's house with." She laughed, never seeming to tire of the fact that I had blown up that tree. I got the strong impression that she was what Gus always liked to call me: "Ornery." Maybe I got my orneriness from her.

The cane felt light in my hand, and just as I'd come so alive on the Rockefeller Center ice, I felt vibrant and powerful with the wooden staff in my grip. I twirled the cane slowly, standing so I didn't bop Grandmother on the nose. The cane bounced and quivered in my hand. I twirled it faster and faster, like a majorette would a baton, something I'd never tried in my life. I flipped it from hand to hand, up in the air, catching it perfectly in mid-spin. I threw it behind my back and caught it with my opposite hand. It seemed to have a life of its own.

Grandmother watched and shook her head. "You're some piece of work, Carol."

I smiled and sat back down, laying the cane across my lap and feeling more than a little pleased with myself. Just holding it made me happy. I decided that if Grandmother was giving it to me to keep, the cane would never leave my sight. "They should let me go with them," I said suddenly. I was about to burst, my body exploding with energy. "I'm soooooo ready." It was like watching someone else say the words. I *never* say things like that.

Grandmother studied me closely. "Maybe," she said. "But, Carol, my sweet, we are never truly ready for our greatest tests. You can prepare and prepare and pre-pare, and then when you're in the thick of it, everything changes. And you have to deal with something you never imagined in a million years."

I nodded, listening to the words but not fully absorbing them. The cane pulsed in my hand. "I'm ready," I repeated, never more sure of anything in my life. I wanted to fight, to protect Santa and the Defenders, to defeat the evil man who had destroyed my friend and taken my father from me. I no longer felt like a misfit, at last finding the place where I belonged, where I mattered. I was beginning to understand the power buried deep within me and what I was capable of. But I should have listened to Grandmother more closely. I should have heeded her words. Perhaps then I would have been better prepared for what was about to happen.

CHAPTER 11

The Gathering

OK, I'll admit it. I pouted most of the day on Christmas Eve. Pretty unattractive, I know, but I couldn't help myself. Gifted One, wise beyond my years, magically powerful, part elf, blah-blah-blah, but I'm still just a twelve-year-old girl. And, hey, we can be moody.

Mrs. Claus tried her best. I told her about my Christmas Eve tradition: Gus would always stop by the house before he'd leave to visit his own family, and we'd bake Christmas cookies and a holiday cake together, listening to Christmas carols, licking the batter off the spoon and then stuffing ourselves with the sweet treats. Uncle Christopher would even try a cookie—just one, of course—and would compliment the chefs before retreating to his study while his staff prepared Christmas Eve dinner. Mrs. Claus and I baked cookies, and it was enjoyable enough—I mean, how can a kid NOT love baking cookies in Santa's house—but I was distracted.

I was so disappointed that Santa and the Defenders were going to leave me behind that night. I guess I thought maybe things had changed. I had trained hard with Dad, getting stronger every day, learning to focus my powers. I could feel those threads of time and space and could control them. I stopped time almost as well as Dad did, and my "North Pulses" were as good, maybe better. (He didn't like to admit it; I think it hurt his pride.) And that was without using the cane Grandmother had given me. I kept that a secret.

"What is that thing?" Dad asked. He reached for it, but I jerked away. I didn't want him touching the cane and maybe feeling its power and taking it from me. He gave me a puzzled look.

"Oh, it's nothing." I laughed, as if I were playing keep-away. I tossed it from hand to hand. "Something Grandmother gave me because she knows how much I love Christmas."

He nodded but gave me a last curious glance. Having not been around for the past seven years of my life, he couldn't tell when I was hiding something. Boy, was I glad of that, because on my way home from my visit with Grandmother after she'd given me the cane, I got a taste of its true power.

I stopped in the field between the reindeer barn and the forest that led to the ice kingdom. I made sure no one was watching. Then I waved my hand through the air as Dad had taught me, gathering power. I held the cane in front of me, directing my energies into the piece of striped wood. A lone pine tree stood in the middle of the field, and I thrust the point of the cane in the tree's direction. First came the noise, like a violent crack of lightning as electricity rips through the sky. Then that poor tree just exploded into a thousand bits of needle and twig and bark. Holy moly! I heard shouts in the distance, and I ran and hid behind the barn until the coast was clear. Later that night I heard talk among the Defenders about the "strange lightning strike" that blew up the tree. I kept my head down and my mouth shut. I caught Dad and Mr. Winters watching me curiously. Surely they had sensed the surge of Defender power. But thankfully no one said anything.

Anyway, back to the pouting. I'm really quite skilled at it. Though my uncle had always been just as skilled at ignoring me. But Gus and the rest of the staff? Not so much. I managed to get my way most of the time or scam some ice cream out of Gus if I was "in a mood." Dad, however, was more like my uncle. "Quit being a baby, Carol," he told me after I'd begged him, yet again, to let me go and then crossed my arms and stomped when he refused. (I'm not proud of myself.)

"Grandmother thinks the Masked Man's going to attack," I said. "And I can help."

"Maybe," he said. "But I'm not about to take the chance of something happening to you. I would never forgive myself."

"And what if something happens to you and I could have stopped it? How do you think I'll feel?"

He pulled me into a hug. "Nothing's going to happen to me, Carol."

"It did before."

"But this time I'm not alone. When the Defenders work together, they're a powerful team. And there's just one of him."

"He has at least two Defenders working for him, plus the magic staff Grandmother told us about!"

"We can handle it," Dad said firmly. "Now please, Carol, I have to prepare for tonight." I nodded, trying to pull in my lower lip, at least till he was out of sight.

And then I was the Useless One again. I didn't visit Grandmother because I would see her that night. She had invited me to something called The Gathering. So after I finished baking cookies, I sat on the front porch in full Pout Mode, watching the comings and goings of elves and Defenders and Santa and Mrs. Claus. The elves polished Santa's sleigh till it shone like a cherry red sports car. The reindeer were brushed and exercised and fed. The Defenders checked the deer they would be riding, chatting as they prepared for the big night. Santa oversaw it all, and Mrs. Claus darted from elf to Defender to me to Santa, offering hot chocolate and the cookies we'd baked. She also snuck me homemade vanilla ice cream made from pristine North Pole snow (which, at least for a few minutes, took me out of Pout Mode).

Bored, I wandered over to the toy factory after lunch and was shocked by the sight. Every elf in the ice kingdom, except for the few tending to the reindeer, must have been there. It was a madhouse. Toys were being sent through a giant contraption that had a long conveyor belt, claw arms, and metal prongs sticking out every which way. It sort of looked like an assembly line at a car factory. Down the conveyor belt the toys would go. Different claws grabbed different size gifts, placing them on a flat metal surface onto which large pieces of colorful wrapping paper were slid. Metal bars shot up and pushed the wrapping paper around the gifts. Then another arm, basically a giant tape dispenser, sealed each package. The wrapped package slid to the ribbon station, and bows were slapped on at lightning speed. Next was the labeling station where an elf sat with a master list, typing in names as each gift slid by, the machine spitting out labels. Another elf double-checked each label against his own list, then applied it to the gift. From there each present was placed in giant rolling bins marked by town, country, and continent. The process was a wonder to behold.

I watched for a while, hypnotized by the whirring and clanging, when all of the elves suddenly gathered near the end of the line. A final present reached the labeling station, and once it had its label, the machine was turned off and everything fell silent. The elf with the master list double-checked the label, nodded triumphantly, and carried it to a bin marked New Zealand. He placed it gently on top of the pile of presents, smiled broadly, and then stepped back. I heard in my head: *The last toy!* The elves clapped, a soft pitter-patter of delicate hands. Some hugged. One even danced a jig. A year's work, finally complete, with only hours to spare. The elves, it seemed, were ready for Christmas.

The gnawing in my gut began during dinner. The time drew near for Santa and the Defenders to leave, and I couldn't quit thinking about Grandmother's prediction that the Masked Man was about to try something. I had moved past pouting and now was in full-fledged Worry Mode. Throughout my two weeks at the North Pole, I had placed Christmas Eve on a back shelf in my mind, kind of like when you know a dentist's appointment is coming and there's going to be drilling involved. You try hard not to dwell on it. But the day had finally come, and all I could think about was the danger they faced, the Masked Man out there, waiting.

After dinner I sat on the front porch swing and watched the final preparations. The elves tethered the reindeer to the sleigh and loaded Santa's initial batch of presents high on the back. Another elf with a list checked off names as Santa's sack was filled. The Defenders inspected the bridles on their reindeer, and I thought of Ramon and how he'd never see another Christmas, never see another Three Kings Day in the Dominican Republic. I tried to push those sad thoughts away and focus on the Defenders. Some had saddles, others rode bareback, depending on their skill as a rider. Dad preferred no saddle, and though I was frightened for him, I watched with pride as he consulted with Santa over every detail. Santa trusted him and depended on him.

Mr. Winters noticed me sitting on the swing and strolled over. "Good evening, m'lady."

"Hi," I said unenthusiastically. I rocked slowly, the swing squeaking in a gentle rhythm.

"So rumor has it you're an elf," Mr. Winters said and laughed. "I must say, m'lady, that caught me by surprise."

"Well, part elf, I guess. And a bunch of generations removed."

"Ah, but that explains so much. It appears your Defender and elf blood make for a powerful mix."

"Then why can't I go? I'm worried about you all. I'm worried about Dad."

Mr. Winters sat on the swing beside me. "He loves you, Carol," he said softly. "He worships the ground you walk on. He wants to protect you."

I sighed. "I know."

"I will watch out for him, m'lady. That will be my sacred mission." Mr. Winters leaned closer. "You want to know a secret?"

I nodded.

"I've never told this to another soul." He looked around to see if any Defenders were listening. "The reason I do the whole 'm'lady' and 'm'lord' thing is that I think of the Defenders as knights, like King Arthur's Knights of the Round Table. Only Santa is our king. Is that weird?"

"Maybe a little," I said and smiled at him. "And you call *everybody* m'lord and m'lady."

He smiled back. "Just habit, I guess. So then, *m'lady*, I

want you to consider me a gallant knight who is forever in your service." Mr. Winters got up and knelt before me as a knight would before his queen.

I couldn't help but giggle. He was the oddest person I'd ever met, but I really cared about him and he really cared about me. I grabbed my cane, standing to play along, and announced, "I hereby knight you Sir Winters of the North Pole!" I tapped him lightly on the shoulder. The cane pulsed, and Mr. Winters jolted. He must have felt the energy coursing through him.

He smiled and said, "You never cease to amaze me, Christmas Carol." He stood and bowed grandly. "I will not fail you, m'lady. You have my word." And my gallant knight marched off to battle.

I didn't want to let my father go. We were hugging just as darkness settled. The pang in my gut had only grown sharper after Santa and all of us Defenders had stood in a circle, holding hands and powering up. As Santa boarded his sleigh and the Defenders saddled up, I clung to Dad.

"Carol, honey, I have to go," he said gently. "Don't worry, we'll be careful. I love you bunches, OK, Angel Butt?" He smiled at me sweetly.

"I love you, too, Daddy."

He bent down and kissed my cheek. I stepped back and watched him climb onto his reindeer, a powerful animal with a distinctive white spot around his left eye. Mrs. Claus materialized beside me and put her arm around my shoulder. I wondered how many times she had watched her husband fly off on Christmas Eve. He had always returned safe and sound. I had to have faith that this time would be no different.

"Ready, Defenders?" Santa yelled.

"Ready!" they called in unison, a thunderous response that made me feel better. There was real power in their unity.

"Then away we fly," Santa called, snapping the reins to his team. The reindeer reared at the crack of leather. Then as one they lunged forward, running hard across the yard and taking off into the night sky. The Defenders followed, each waving. Mr. Winters yelled, "Back soon, m'lady." My father was the last to go. He blew me a kiss and mouthed the words, "I love you." I mouthed the same words back, and up he went, soaring into the darkness.

Mrs. Claus squeezed my shoulder. "You want to come inside for hot cocoa, dear?" she asked. "Or are you going to The Gathering?"

I looked at her, surprised. "How did you know?"

"I thought they might invite you. The elves seem to have taken a liking to you."

"What goes on there?" I asked. Grandmother had acted all mysterious, not explaining much about it.

"The elves gather every Christmas Eve. Some send the toys through the portal, working in shifts because it's a very long night. The others just watch, I think, though I'm not entirely sure. It's an honor to be invited. I never have been."

This I knew. Grandmother said some elves objected to my being invited. No human had ever witnessed The Gathering. ("We elves just *love* the melodramatic names," she joked, rolling her eyes.) But the elf king and queen had granted special permission for the Gifted One to come. I would report to them at the toy factory, where

The Gathering was to take place. "I could ask if you can come, too," I said to Mrs. Claus.

"No, dear. You go. Tell me all about it afterward. I must say I am curious, but it wouldn't be right for me to intrude." She smiled and squeezed my shoulder once more, and we went our separate ways, each of us anticipating a long and nervous night of waiting for the ones we loved.

All the elves in the kingdom—hundreds and hundreds of them—must have been there. Tents had been set up outside the toy factory, and elves gathered around tables filled with every kind of food and drink imaginable. Elf children played games. There was laughter and music and dancing. It was odd to hear such merriment from the elves, who usually communicated so silently. The Gathering was not at all what I had imagined. I had pictured a solemn event; this was a party.

Some of the elves noticed my arrival, and the whispers began. I suspected not all of them had gotten the message that I could hear their thoughts. *What's she doing here? Who invited her? No humans allowed!* Or maybe they knew about my ability and *wanted* me to hear. Grandmother certainly heard. She suddenly appeared, loud and angry in my head and theirs. *BE QUIET, ALL OF YOU! I INVITED HER.* The voices ceased. I saw bowed heads and sheepish looks. Grandmother led me into the heart of The Gathering. *Don't mind them,* she said. She raised her voice again—or however you would describe making her telepathy louder. *THEY'RE SILLY CREATURES WHO CAN'T DEAL WITH THE SLIGHTEST BIT OF CHANGE!*

"I don't want to cause any trouble," I said aloud.

"Nonsense. You are my guest. And if what I suspect is true, by the end of the night they will be happy you're here."

"What do you mean?"

"Never mind that now. Are you hungry?" I shook my head no. With my stomach so tied in knots, I couldn't imagine putting food into it. "All right then. To the portal we go. The king and queen await."

We walked along the edge of the factory where I'd watched the final toys come off the assembly line, and when we rounded the corner, I was stunned to see what most definitely had not been there a few hours before. At the end of the building, where the doors were flung wide open to bring out the bins of packages, stood a massive structure made of ice. It looked sort of like one of those magnifying mirrors you see in hotel bathrooms. There were two columns of thick ice on each side, and hanging in the middle was a giant circle of ice. Where the mirror would have been was empty air. "The portal vessel," Grandmother said.

Beside the vessel stood two stunningly beautiful creatures with long, white hair that flowed around their red robes. Their faces were as pale as the moon and glowed just as brightly, more so than any of the elves I had encountered. Their eyes were blue ice, cold and deep and full of mystery. If you want the truth, they scared me a little. They wore no crowns, but I guessed who they were before Grandmother said: *My king, my queen, I present to you the Gifted One.*

They were so beautiful that I wasn't sure which was which. The elf on the right was larger, his face slightly more masculine, so I assumed he had to be the king. But it was the queen who addressed me first, stepping forward. *Come closer, my child.* Her voice in my head was soft and kind, and when she smiled, her beauty made me tremble. A power radiated from her, an inner strength. As I stepped toward her, I wondered what it would be like to be such an extraordinary creature.

But you are, my child, the queen said. *And what's within you is more powerful than you can ever know.*

I don't feel that way, I said, chagrined that I had revealed my thoughts to her.

Then you are foolish, she said, not unkindly. *Always remember that you are an extraordinary girl who will grow to be an extraordinary woman. You are the master of your fate.*

I bowed awkwardly, and Grandmother gave her usual grunt. "Too old to bow," she grumbled.

We are about to begin, Carol, the king said. *We are honored to have the Gifted One at The Gathering. It is the culmination of our yearlong purpose, a celebration of all we've accomplished and the joy we help spread around the world.*

"Cool," I responded, unsure of what to say but pretty sure *that* wasn't it.

The king smiled. *Yes, very cool.* He turned to the giant

ice structure. The queen walked to the other side of it. Massive bins of gifts had been pulled close by the reindeer, each of them being ridden by an elf. The bins nearest to the structure were marked NEW ZEALAND, where night first fell on the earth. The king raised his hands. The queen raised hers, too. The Gathering fell silent. The elves closed their eyes, even Grandmother. I started to but changed my mind. I wanted to see what was happening. I was of no help anyway, since I didn't have a clue what they were about to do. Once again, the Useless One. There was a low hum, and I realized it came from the elves, their voices one long, drawn-out note. The hum never paused, and I wondered how they were able to maintain that note and still breathe.

Electricity crackled in the air. What looked like tiny bolts of lightning shot across the empty space of the ice circle. The humming grew louder. The air in the circle flickered and pulsed. An image began to form. The humming was so loud it began to hurt my ears. I put my hands up to cover them, and just like that, the humming stopped, the elves' eyes popped open in unison, the king and queen put down their hands, and there was Santa, as plain as if he were right in front of us. The Defenders flew in formation around the sleigh. The image drew close, as if we were looking through a video camera and someone was pressing ZOOM. I caught a glimpse of my father, then Mr. Winters. None of them seemed aware they were being watched. Santa glanced toward us and gave a slight nod. Our view swung around to the back of the sleigh where two elves were perched next to the stacks of presents. The image zoomed in tight on the elves and that's where it stayed. One of the elves waved. The king waved back. He turned to the elves who were on the reindeer pulling the bins, motioning for them to spur the deer close to the portal. Then we waited.

I watched, fascinated by the idea that Santa was on the other side of the world, somewhere over New Zealand, and the elves were about to hand him packages. So cool! I heard Santa say, "Whoa!" and the sleigh bumped to a stop. I turned to Grandmother and said, *I thought you couldn't hear through a portal.*

This is The Gathering portal. Only through our combined powers can we create one this strong.

The elves with Santa asked, *Ready?* Then an answer. *Ready!* And a group of elves on our side lined up and began passing presents from one to the next, the elf stand-ing closest to the portal tossing the package through. I noticed he kept well back. *He can't reach in?* I asked.

He would be pulled through to where Santa is. And portals are one way, so if he tried to come back through, he'd be sucked into oblivion, which would be rather unfortunate.

It was the strangest thing, watching the packages being transported. The elf would toss the present in, and the eyes of the elf on the other side would follow the flight of the package. There would be a three-second pause, and then he'd reach out and catch it. Again and again, an elf would toss from our side, three-second delay, catch. Toss, delay, catch. We watched for what seemed like an eternity. There would be breaks while Santa traveled to his next stop. The elves doing the tossing would get a drink, and maybe a piece of candy or a cookie. But then it would start all over again, more bins rolled out and more toys tossed through.

After a while, if you must know, I got bored, my legs cramping from standing still so long. I wondered how Grandmother could endure it, as old as she was. Naturally, she heard my thoughts, and I was embarrassed. *I'm fine, my sweet. We're built for this. Time moves much slower for us. Go get yourself a treat. But stay close. I may need you.*

For what?

Just do as I ask, please. Her voice sounded impatient, and I cringed. *I must concentrate,* she said, gentler this time.

OK, I said. I made my way through the elves. Except for the ones unloading the toys, not a single elf moved. Every elf at The Gathering stood and stared at the portal, as if hypnotized. Honestly, it creeped me out. They looked like they were in some kind of trance and didn't act like they even knew I was there.

I meandered back to where the food was set up. In our visits, Grandmother had offered an array of elfin treats. "Sweets for my sweet," she would say. My favorite was a gummy-like candy, always red or green, that she jokingly called "our power pills." They did seem to give you a burst of energy, and, obviously, I liked the colors. It was going to be a long night, so I grabbed a handful and stuffed them into my jacket pocket.

I wandered over to a seat that resembled a lounge lawn chair but was made of ice and gave me a clear view of the portal. I leaned back and popped a few "power pills," which made me feel warm and fuzzy, instead of giving me an energy boost. I laid my cane across my lap and watched the portal, hoping to catch a glimpse of my father or Mr. Winters. But all I could see was the endless parade of presents. My eyes grew heavy. I shook myself a few times, trying to stay awake for whatever task Grandmother would ask of me. But I didn't hold out long. Like children all over the world on Christmas Eve, I drifted off to sleep.

The next thing I knew I was startled awake by a horrible sound, a wrenching in my mind, like tearing metal. I sat up in a panic and wiped drool from the corner of my mouth. It took a second to remember where I was. But when I did, what I saw horrified me. As far as the eye could see, elves lay motionless. And silent. The portal was gone. The bins of toys sat lined up, one after the other, the reindeer waiting patiently to be guided. But no elves were awake to do so. Even the king and queen lay sprawled on the ground. Were they unconscious? Dead? I leaped to my feet, the cane clattering to the ground. I reached down to pick it up and heard a faint voice in my head, *Carol, my child. Help.*

I raced to where Grandmother lay among the elves. "Oh, no!" I said, my voice piercing the silence like a gunshot. I squatted next to her. "Are you hurt? What happened?"

"He came," Grandmother said weakly, and I didn't have to ask who. The Masked Man. "He destroyed the portal. He cut us off." I helped her sit up.

"What about Dad? Santa?"

"I don't know. I heard screams, so I disengaged from the portal. I sensed what was coming. The rest . . ." she looked at the downed elves, " . . . they were all connected when the portal was destroyed. It was too much for them." The elves were breathing, but their eyes were wide open, as if in shock.

"What do we do?" I asked.

"Not me. You." She pointed to my cane. "Use it. Make a portal. Go to them."

I looked at where the portal had been and at the stunned elves, and that gnawing in my gut spread through my body. I felt like I might be sick. "But I'm afraid," I said. For all my begging of my father to take me with them, for all the boasting I had done to Grandmother that I was ready, now that the reality of the Masked Man was before me, my body trembled.

"You should be, my sweet," Grandmother said softly. "But still you must go. They need you." She pointed to the ice ring. "Think of your father. Your connection with him is the strongest. Then focus the energy into the cane and point it toward the vessel. I will help as best I can."

I nodded and stood. I closed my eyes and held the cane in front of me. I thought of my dad and him teasing me and calling me Angel Butt. I imagined the feel of his arms when he hugged me goodbye. I pictured him mouthing the words, "I love you," as he flew off. A tear rolled down my cheek. I whispered, "I love you, too," trying to tap into the deep power of my emotion. I could feel the energy gathering, like storm clouds in my mind, stronger than I'd ever felt, even stronger than when I destroyed that poor pine tree in the field. I opened my eyes and aimed the cane at the center of the ring, keeping Dad's face in my mind. For good measure, I thought of Mr. Winters and him together, two men I knew as well as any on Earth. The ring pulsed with electricity, the air shimmering. The image slowly came into focus, and what I saw was terrifying. The

Masked Man gazed back at me, directly into the portal. Santa and his sleigh were in the background. The enemy hovered on his flying machine. His body convulsed with rage at the sight of me, and he aimed his staff in my direction. "Now, Carol!" Grandmother screamed, and I ran as hard as I could toward the portal, closed my eyes, and dove through. Only then did it occur to me that I had no reindeer.

CHAPTER 12

Facing the Enemy

I couldn't breathe, and time seemed to slow to a halt as I traveled through whatever dimension the portal had created. It was stifling hot, like a muggy, humid Florida day. I felt as if I were underwater, the world distorted into a fun house mirror. Behind me I saw a stretched-out version of Grandmother, as if she were twenty feet tall and made of Silly Putty. I looked ahead, and the Masked Man was wider than a fat lady at an old-time circus freak show. I felt disoriented. Sick to my stomach. I felt stuck.

I heard a voice in my head, faint at first. *Kick, Carol.* Then louder. Grandmother. *Like you're swimming. Kick!* I kicked my feet in unison and felt myself move. I kicked harder, the Masked Man getting closer. Only now he was thin in the middle and fat up top, his head like some kind of super-brained, big-skulled creature in a sci-fi movie. He looked even scarier that way. I kicked three more times with all my might. The Masked Man turned away from me and grew smaller, and I wondered if that were another trick of the portal. Surely he wasn't running from me.

Then I was through. The cold night air jolted me but felt good after being inside the sweltering portal. I was high in the wispy clouds. The bright moon lit up the landscape far below. Mountains blanketed by endless trees rolled beneath me. I hung in the air for a moment, as if the portal still held me in its grip, and then I started to fall. So stupid! Here I was rushing in to save the day, only to plummet to my death. Truly the Useless One.

Above me I saw Santa and his sleigh being chased by the Masked Man. No, the enemy hadn't been running from me. Santa was his target, not some silly girl. Two other men on flying machines hovered on either side of the Masked Man. The traitorous ex-Defenders, I guessed! The true Defenders swarmed around Santa, forming a shield. A combined pulse of immense power blasted out of their formation, and the Masked Man was knocked back. He was stunned. The traitors were blown from the sky, disappearing as they plunged to the earth. A victory!

The battle disappeared into the clouds as I rocketed toward Earth. I felt so helpless, so stupid and useless. But then I heard an odd noise, like the sucking sound a boot makes when it's pulled out of deep mud. I looked up at the portal. Out popped a reindeer, darting through the air. Grandmother had sent the deer through to me! "Down here," I yelled, and the deer dove toward me, like a jet screaming through the night, catching up to me in an instant and slowing as it flew under my legs. I landed on the reindeer's back with a thump. "Haaaa!" I shouted, spurring on my mount. The reindeer shot ahead. The chase was on.

I zipped through the sky toward where I'd last seen the battle. All was quiet now, the silence ominous. Had the Masked Man already won? I tried not to think about what that could mean for me, for Mrs. Claus. Had we lost the ones we loved? Had the world lost Santa? Suddenly a riderless reindeer shot toward me, its eyes ablaze with terror. I recognized that deer, the white spot around his left eye, no saddle on his back. My stomach dropped, and I thought I might be sick. My father's deer. "No!" I screamed and spurred my reindeer on. "Faster! Faster!"

I bent low, my face behind the head of the reindeer, my cane gripped in one hand, the reins in the other. Tears cut warm paths down my cold cheeks. I heard the whir of the Masked Man's machine. Beyond him I saw Santa's sleigh, the Masked Man in pursuit. As I drew nearer, the enemy seemed unaware of my presence. I sat up high on the reindeer's back and let go of the reins, squeezing tight with my legs. I closed my eyes and concentrated, waving my hand through the cool night air, gathering my power. I focused the gathered energy into the wooden cane, tapping into its ancient elfin magic. With a fierce scream, I flung the point at the Masked Man. The air trembled like the ground in an earthquake. The blast slammed the Masked Man forward. He tumbled from his flying machine, toward the mountains below. His machine spun out of control, following him toward the ground. The Masked Man cartwheeled through the air and fell and fell, until I could no longer see him. There was silence.

I couldn't believe it! He was gone. I beat him! I searched frantically for my father. Santa stood up in his sleigh and waved. I heard Mr. Winters calling from afar, "Carol! Carol! Over here." He appeared on his reindeer, circling from behind Santa's sleigh. On the back of the deer, his arms around Mr. Winters's waist, sat my father. A wave of relief washed over me. I flew toward them. "I promised you I'd protect him, didn't I, m'lady?" Mr. Winters hollered. The Defenders cheered, yelling, "Good job!" The elves on Santa's sleigh said, *Thank you, Gifted One. You saved us.* Santa tipped his red and white cap.

"Carol, what are you doing here?" my father asked, but he was smiling broadly.

"Saving our bacon, I believe," Mr. Winters said. They flew toward me. I wanted to hug my father, to hug Mr. Winters. But before I could reach them, a panicked voice cut through the night air. Santa yelled, "Look out!" I whirled. And there he was, the Masked Man, floating toward us without his machine. He pointed his staff below him and the air shimmered. Somehow he was creating invisible waves that pushed him upward, like the blast from a rocket.

"You didn't think it would be that easy, did you, little girl?" the Masked Man said. He spoke through a device that disguised his voice. The sound was vaguely robotic. Twisted and evil. I felt paralyzed, terrified. He raised his staff and hurled a mighty blast. Had I not put up my cane as a shield, that might have been the end for me. The air felt alive, then solid as a punch, a giant fist that slammed into me. The breath escaped my lungs. My deer and I tumbled backward. I held onto the reins, hanging from the deer as we somersaulted toward Earth.

"No!" my father yelled, and he and Mr. Winters went on the attack. More Defenders zoomed in from every direction. "As one!" Mr. Winters shouted, and they concentrated their power into a mighty blast. The air trembled, and the blast was so strong it flung my father and Mr. Winters backward, like the kick of a shotgun, both of them clinging to the deer. The Masked Man reeled.

I watched as I fell. I yanked hard on the reins, but my deer seemed dazed. I pulled myself onto his back and placed my hand on his head, concentrating my energy into him. The deer stirred, but we kept falling. I could see mountains below, approaching fast. I turned my body toward the earth and aimed my power toward the ground, as I'd seen the Masked Man do. We slowed to a halt, just a few feet from a field covered by patches of snow. My deer's legs started to churn. I wondered where we were. Not that it mattered. Whatever this place was, it would not be where I would die.

Up, up I flew. I couldn't see the battle but heard the boom of North Pulses. "Faster!" I yelled, but my deer seemed to be injured, flying at half speed. I could hear his ragged breath. I heard another huge blast, and the clouds above me parted, revealing the battle.

Then it happened, the worst thing I could ever imagine. The Masked Man hovered. The Defenders and Santa were arrayed in formation in front of him. I heard a hum, a great power building and building. The Masked Man seemed to slow. He held his staff high above his head, as if he were drawing power from the moon itself. The Defenders and Santa froze. I thought they were preparing their own attack, but then I realized they couldn't move. The Masked Man brought his staff forward with such tremendous speed that I could barely see it. A huge blast burst forth from his weapon, like the waves of power you see in the films of nuclear bomb tests, everything in the path annihilated. The Defenders and Santa were helpless, and they were flung backward. Santa's sleigh overturned, throwing him and the elves and the packages into the air. I heard grunts and cries of pain. Santa's sleigh splintered and broke into a thousand pieces. His team of reindeer fell toward Earth. Defenders were tossed from their mounts. Santa, my father, the Defenders, and elves—they were all unconscious, lifeless, falling, falling, falling. I tried freezing them, but I was too far away, my deer too weak to get me there in time.

The Masked Man had won. I had failed. I lost my friends. I lost Santa Claus. I lost my father again, this time for good.

A fury rose inside me. Grief and anger and pain swirled as I watched them disappear into the black night. "AAAAIIIIEEEHHHHH!" I screamed, and something stirred within me. It was a power so deep, so strong, I felt as if my body might explode. The universe trembled. The Masked Man spun to face me.

"You're a monster!" I screamed, and my words sounded far away, as if they belonged to someone else, some out-of-body version of me.

"I am victorious," he said in his robotic voice. He laughed. "And you are just a girl in way over her head."

Then the words came back to me, the ones weird Mr. Winters had spoken to me at Rockefeller Center, where he first revealed that I had a greater purpose. *A girl is a powerful, powerful thing. Never doubt your worth.* I heard the words the queen had said to me just hours before. *Always remember that you are an extraordinary girl . . . You are the master of your fate.* The anger roiled within me. My body glowed. My hair stood on end. The white strand hung in my face, blazing like hot steel. I brushed it aside with my left hand and raised the cane with my right. "I am NOT just a girl," I yelled. "I am a Defender of Claus!"

The Masked Man laughed again. "Silly child. There's no one left to defend." He raised his staff, preparing his final attack. The weapon vibrated with power. He pulled it back to hurl his next pulse, the one that would end me, that would complete his triumph. But suddenly he stopped. He froze in place, as if stricken with fear. For a second I was confused, but then I realized I was the one doing it. I felt myself rise. I don't know where the power came from, but I began to float above my deer. The Masked Man hung in the air, unmoving. I pulled the cane tight to my chest. I started to spin, slowly at first, then faster and faster, until everything was a blur. It felt like I had no control over my body, yet I was controlling everything. My rage fueled the strength.

I spun so fast I could hardly see. I felt the power building within me until I was about to burst. I thought about the Defender of old who had lost control of his power and vanished. "Poof," Mr. Winters had said. But I didn't care. If I vanished, so be it. I didn't want to live in a world without my father, a world without Santa Claus. I craved every ounce of energy I could gather. When I didn't think I could take it anymore, I willed myself to stop. My body pulsed with energy. I felt electrified, tiny bolts of lightning firing from every one of my wide-open pores. The cane sizzled. I held my left hand to my face, and it glowed, sparks of electricity passing between my fingers. I extended the cane with my right. I moved my left hand forward, and my deer and the Masked Man moved forward with it. I moved it backward, as if I were tugging at the air itself, and they moved backward as well. I did it again, forward then back. Then an idea hit me so hard I gasped.

I started pulling, grabbing the strings of the universe. My deer lurched backward, heading down from where it had come. The Masked Man jerked back, spinning away from me but entirely in my control. The threads of time and space crisscrossed in a massive silvery grid before me, a web I could touch and manipulate, and I hoped that what I thought was happening was actually happening.

I kept pulling and pulling, but nothing appeared for what seemed like the longest time. I began to lose hope. Maybe it wasn't possible. Perhaps what was done was done. But then, far below, came a black speck in the gray, moonlit sky. Then came another speck. And another. Then I saw a spot of red. Santa! I pulled as hard as I could, string after string of time itself. Then they appeared, my father and Mr. Winters. Their bodies reversed the tumble they had taken. The sounds of the battle and their screams were like a song played backward. Santa drew closer, the elves somersaulting beside him. The shattered sleigh pieced itself back together, with the strange sound of unsplintering wood. The reindeer straightened into their usual line, and Santa and his elves and the packages dropped back into the reconstructed sleigh. The other Defenders retraced the paths of their falls and landed safely atop their mounts. My father and Mr. Winters were the last

hand in response. With such power throbbing within me, all it took was a flick of my fingers to freeze him. He struggled against me. I heard him grunting under the mask, summoning every ounce of energy to break free. I floated serenely toward him. I glanced back at Mr. Winters and my father, who watched with mouths open. I stopped in front of the Masked Man, hovering before him, studying the demonic mask and his magic staff. I felt him trying to move his mouth to speak. I relaxed my power so that he could. "Who do you think you are to oppose me?" he barked. His robotic voice no longer sounded frightening.

I floated closer, nose to nose. I smiled, looking into the eyes peering out from the mask. I could see his fear. I whispered, "Who do I think I am? I am Christmas Carol." Then I ripped the mask from his face.

I will always regret what happened next. I should have been more focused. I should have taken his staff, maybe tied him up. I should have asked the Defenders to help subdue him. But I let my guard down for just a second. That second was when the mask fell away, and the man underneath was revealed. That was the longest second of my life, when everything I thought I knew about the past six years of my existence was shattered. Floating before me was the last person on Earth I expected to see.

Uncle Christopher.

Maybe some of you saw this coming. Maybe you weren't as blind as I was. Yes, my uncle could be ruthless and greedy. He could be cold and impatient and act as if I were a burden. But he had always provided for me, taking me in when there was no one else. I loved my uncle, warts and all. For the longest time, he was the only family I had. I never would have suspected him in a million years.

But as it dawned on me that he was the Masked Man, the enemy who had kidnapped my father (his own brother!), killed Ramon, destroyed Santa and the Defenders, and had turned to destroy me next, I lost my focus.

"Carol, dear," my uncle snarled, his voice deep and cold and chillingly evil. "You . . . will . . . pay . . . for this." The last word came out like a hiss. The words shook me. I lost my hold on him. I floated backward, too shocked to function, staring at the man who had red hair and a white stripe, just like I did, but had concealed the mark of the Defender and used his powers for evil. My uncle, *the enemy*, saw his chance. He belted me with a North Pulse.

I tumbled backward, the air knocked from my lungs. I struggled to breathe. My ears rang. Pain knifed through my brain. As I fell, my uncle raised his weapon again. I thought he was going to launch another attack, finish me off, and then go after Santa once more. But instead, he created a portal directly in front of him. It shimmered and sputtered and then came into focus. I saw palm trees, a beach. The Defenders rushed to stop him, but he dove through. The portal closed behind him, with a pop. And just like that, he was gone.

I plummeted toward Earth, too exhausted and too shattered to care. But then my body jerked to a halt. I floated upside down. My father and Mr. Winters flew to me.

"Carol!" my dad called. "Are you all right?" I hung in the air where they had frozen me. I felt woozy and nauseated. Mr. Winters grabbed the reins of my deer, which had flown back up to us, and guided him to me. They set me gently on the reindeer's back, and I slumped against his neck. My father climbed on and pulled me to his chest. His warmth enveloped me. I've had some good hugs in my life, but without a doubt, that was the best one ever. "Thank you, Carol," he said softly. "Thank you."

"Did you see, Daddy?" I was sobbing now. "Did you see who it was?"

"Yes, honey."

"How could he? How could he do that?"

"I don't know, sweetheart." Dad kissed the top of my head and whispered that it would be all right. Santa and the Defenders and the elves watched in silence. And time stood still.

So you might think saving Santa Claus, rescuing my father and the rest of the Defenders, and defeating the enemy were the most amazing things I did on Christmas Eve. Well, maybe. Kind of hard to top that. But I felt so betrayed it was impossible to feel triumph. And the fact that my uncle had escaped ruined any celebration. But Santa let me do something later that night that lifted my spirits.

The battle had been fought over the mountains of West Virginia. When the Masked Man attacked, Santa had been about to deliver toys to the children of a little town called Petersburg. Now that the enemy had been defeated, Santa still had a job to do.

The Defenders were congratulating me. "You are ever full of surprises, m'lady," Mr. Winters said, hugging me tightly.

"We owe you a great debt," Santa said, putting his arm around my shoulders.

"It was nothing," I said, proud but embarrassed by the attention. And I was still mad at myself for letting my uncle get away. A voice popped into my head. *Carol, my sweet!* I turned to see a crackle of electricity in the air, then the blurry image of elves rising from the ground. Grandmother and the king and queen stood, concentrating on the other side of the portal. The portal sizzled and popped, then *bam!* Crystal clear. I watched more elves pick themselves up, shaking their heads to clear the cobwebs. They joined their comrades in concentrating on the restored portal. Grandmother smiled and waved. *I'm so proud of you, my child. We all are.* The king, the queen, and all the elves smiled at me. Grandmother had been right. Now the elves were definitely glad I had come to The Gathering. *Thank you, Gifted One . . . You saved us . . . We are forever grateful.*

You're welcome, I said, blushing.

"OK, Defenders," Santa interrupted. "Back to work." He turned to me. "Carol, my dear. You ride beside me." He patted the seat next to him. My father nudged the reindeer close to the sleigh, and I climbed in. I sat down, trying to process the fact that I was about to fly with Santa Claus to help deliver toys on Christmas Eve! Good gravy, that was nuts. "Away!" Santa yelled, and the reindeer zipped into the night, carrying us down to the good children of Petersburg.

That's how we spent the rest of Christmas Eve: Darting from house to house, the Defenders stopping time, the elves tossing presents through the portal, Santa popping in and out of homes delivering gifts. Between stops, Santa and I rode in silence. I didn't much feel like talking, even though I knew I should be thrilled at getting to ride in the sleigh. Santa watched me out of the corner of his eye, concern on his face. "What troubles you, my dear?" he finally asked.

I sighed. "I can't stop thinking about him. I should have figured it out. I keep thinking about that shadow I saw moving at Rockefeller Center while everyone was frozen. That must have been my uncle."

"You may be right."

"Where do you think he is now?"

"Somewhere licking his wounds, I suppose," Santa said. "We will have to remain vigilant. I don't think this is the last we'll hear from him."

"So you didn't have any idea that he had Defender powers? That *he* was the Masked Man?"

Santa thought for a moment. "Not really. He must have dyed his hair to hide the white stripe. But now that I know, it makes sense."

"Why?

"Your uncle was always greedy, even as a child. No matter how he acted—and let's just say he could be pretty naughty—he always asked for twice as much for Christmas as his brother. One year, when he was particularly naughty, I gave him just one gift, plus a lump of coal in his stocking."

"Coal?" Then it clicked in my brain. The polished black rock with the International Toy logo! "He still has that!" I said, describing the carved rock and how Uncle Christopher always kept it on his desk at work and even took it to New York City with him.

"That doesn't surprise me," Santa said. "I bet he kept it as a reminder of what I did to him."

"But he deserved it if he was bad," I said.

"I guess he didn't see it that way. Greed has a way of blinding people, and he became even greedier as an adult. He's forced many of his competitors out of business and keeps raising prices on all his toys." I thought of the angry, little man who confronted my uncle at the toy convention. I wondered if that man had once supplied dolls to Santa. "Then we dropped him and started buying from his biggest competitor. Maybe he found out I was behind that and it was just one more reason to hate me: I was taking money from his pocket."

"But he's already so rich," I said. "I don't understand it."

"I don't think it's just about the money, Carol. It's about power and control, taking over other companies, ruling the entire toy business. There's a saying, 'Power corrupts . . .'"

I finished the sentence before he could. "And absolute power corrupts absolutely." Santa looked at me with surprise. "I learned that from Mr. Winters," I said, grinning. "He's a good teacher, even if he is super weird."

Santa laughed. "Oh, I almost forgot," he said. "I have something for you." He reached into his sack, pulled out a small, beautifully wrapped package, and handed it to me. "You have more presents at the North Pole, of course, but I've been keeping this one with me to give to you personally."

"Thank you, Santa," I said tearing off the wrapping paper and lifting the lid off the box. When I saw what was inside, my heart leaped.

"I know it's a little strange to give you something you already own as a gift," Santa said. "But I know how much it means to you."

Tears pooled in my eyes and I rubbed my fingers over the beautifully painted, hand-carved wooden Santa that my parents had given to me so many years ago, the one I fell asleep gazing at every night, the one I'd been forced to leave behind when I became a Defender. "How did you . . . ?"

"Oh, I have my ways," Santa said, his eyes twinkling. "And that's quite a collection of me you have there. Fifty-nine Santas! My goodness." And he laughed, a real honest-to-goodness "ho-ho-ho" that made his entire body shake with joy. I threw my arms around his neck and buried my face in his thick beard. Santa hugged me back, patting me gently on my head, and on and on we flew.

After a few hours (Defender time, in which virtually no real time passed), I started to get sleepy. Just as I'd done at The Gathering, I fought it, afraid of missing something exciting, afraid everyone would see me as a little kid who couldn't stay up past her bedtime. But exhaustion finally overtook me. Cradling my cane and my wooden Santa, I slumped against the side of the sleigh and slept as deeply as I ever had. What seemed like only a minute later, Santa nudged me awake. I bolted up, startled. It was hot and muggy, and we were still soaring high above the earth. "Where are we?" I asked.

"Hillsboro," Santa said. I had a moment of panic. Were we chasing my uncle, trying to capture him at his home? I felt so tired. I wasn't up for another battle. Santa seemed to read my mind. "We're pretty sure he's not in Hillsboro, sweetheart. I imagine he's at some secret hideaway."

shelf next to the television. Beside it was a tiny plastic Rockefeller Christmas tree, a souvenir from our trip. A glass of milk and a plate with two cookies sat on the living room coffee table. Santa helped himself, and I wondered if he really did eat every single cookie the children put out. I'd have to ask about that later. Four presents sat beneath the sparse tree. Two larger ones were addressed to Amelia's brothers. The third, a small package, read: *To Amelia. Feliz Navidad. Mommy.* And the last, even tinier, read: *To Mommy. Love, Amelia.* That was it. One gift each.

I thought of my own Christmases, and how, in addition to the gifts from Santa, my uncle never failed to get me everything on my list (even if his assistant was the one who actually bought the gifts). I'm not sure why he did it. Maybe it was guilt, knowing what he'd done to my father. Or maybe it was another way for him to compete with Santa Claus, to get back at him for the lump of coal. He could defeat Santa by giving me more presents. But even after everything that had happened, after my uncle's betrayal, there was still no denying the excitement and joy I felt on all those Christmas mornings as I tore into a huge pile of presents and Uncle Christopher watched and occasionally even smiled. Those were good memories.

Getting a bunch of gifts isn't what Christmas is all about. I know that, of course. And I know Amelia had what mattered more: a loving family who would do anything for her. But still, didn't Amelia deserve some of that Christmas joy I'd experienced? Santa watched me as I studied Amelia's tiny gift. I wondered if he could read my thoughts. I assumed he had that ability. But maybe not. Maybe he simply understood me in a way no other adult could. Perhaps that was his true magic: knowing just what every child needs to feel joy, if only once a year.

"A girl worthy of being your best friend must truly be special, Carol," he said softly. He turned his sack over and emptied the whole bag of gifts, dozens of them, onto the floor. I saw several packages addressed to Amelia's brothers. Several more had her mother's name on them. But at least twenty were addressed to Amelia. Many were shaped like books. Lots of "the classics" she so loved, I guessed. Many were from Santa, but when I looked closer, more than a few read: *To: Amelia. From: Carol.*

And on top of all the gifts sat a simple manila folder, addressed to Amelia's father, who was still back in the Dominican Republic. I looked at Santa curiously. He smiled and said, "A little something that will allow him to join his family." I smiled back at him. Of all the gifts Amelia would receive Christmas morning, I knew the one given to someone else would mean the most. I guess *Miracle on 34th Street* wasn't all fantasy. Santa truly could make a family whole. "Ready to go?" he asked.

"Yes," I said, but then paused. "Would it be OK to leave Amelia a note?"

"Certainly, dear. But please hurry."

I nodded and took a pen and notepad from a drawer in the kitchen, sitting down to ponder exactly what I should say. I laid my cane across my lap. My strand of white hair fell across my eye, and I brushed it aside. I put pen to paper.

Dear Amelia,

I don't even know where to begin, but something incredible happened to me. First of all, don't worry. I'm safe. I'm with my dad again. I found him! And I'm going to live with him from now on and we're going to be a family, just like you're going to have a whole family again.

I can't tell you everything that's happened. Some things have to stay secret. But I want you to know I got to visit the Dominican Republic. It was so beautiful, and the people were so wonderful. I absolutely loved it, even though something very sad ended up happening there.

Anyway, just know that I've found my purpose and that Santa Claus is real. I know it sounds crazy, but I was put on this earth to protect him. I never really fit in at Broward. Not like you and your super brain. Mr. Winters helped me discover my true purpose, and he didn't do any of the terrible things I'm sure people accused him of. He's a good man, even if he is really weird.

I need to get going. Santa's waiting on me. Amazing, right? Enjoy all the gifts and say hello to your father for me. I hope to meet him soon. I'll come back to see you someday, I promise. I miss you so much, Amelia. Feliz Navidad.

Love,
Christmas Carol,
Defender of Claus

I stood to go. Santa was slinging his empty sack over his shoulder. Then a thought occurred to me and I quickly sat back down. I knew Santa was eager to leave. It had been a long, harrowing night. Everyone was exhausted and ready to go home. But surely I had earned these few minutes to say what I wanted to say to my best friend. Santa waited patiently. He understood what I needed to do. I picked up the pen again, smiling to myself, thinking about the day I met Amelia and the letter she held so tightly. Under my signature I wrote the words that always made me feel warm inside, words that spoke of the love between a father and a daughter, a love that could be felt from a thousand miles away, or even across time itself. It was a love that Amelia and I had both missed desperately but would have in full once again. I carefully wrote the words that Amelia's *Papi*, in his broken English, always wrote to her:

P.S. I will love you much eternity. Hugs and kisses and butterfly wishes.

I set the pen down and got up to leave. Santa smiled and walked over to put his arm around me. He squeezed me tight, brushed aside the white lock of hair that hung in my eyes and kissed me lightly on the forehead. With a nod of his head and a wave of his hand, we disappeared into the night.

Acknowledgments

I am incredibly lucky to have so many supportive family members and friends, all of whom have been instrumental in one way or another in helping me publish this book. I feel truly blessed.

First off, I want to thank my son, Tyler, who was in the "middle grades" when I started writing this book for him but is now a freshman in high school, something that's almost inconceivable to me. Next up is my wife, Geovanny, who's been incredibly supportive as I try and make my writing dreams come true. I'd also like to thank my parents, Bill and Jodi Fouch, for instilling in me a belief that if you work hard, anything's possible. (I miss you, Dad.) A big thanks to my brother Todd, his wife Heather, and their kids Isaac, Tierra, Ashlee, and Abigail for their encouragement. And a special shout-out to my other son, Richard Feliciano, who continues to make his mother and me proud as he soars through the skies.

I'm also grateful to my *Newsday* pals Kevin Amorim, Jerry Zezima, Jonalyn Schuon, Dan Bubbeo, Gary Rogers, Peggy Brown, Estelle Landers, Ned Levine, Tom Beer, and Thomas Maier for all of their help and advice.

I want to thank Sky Pony for taking a chance on me, and Becky Herrick, my incredible editor, who really pushed me to make the book better. Also, I'm still amazed by illustrator David Miles's magical cover art, which really captured the essence of the book. And last, but certainly not least, I want to thank Bethany Buck, who was the first person in the book industry to truly believe in me and Carol, starting as my agent, then as my editor, and now as just an awesome and supportive friend. I'll be forever in your debt, Bethany.

About the Author

Robert L. Fouch is an author and journalist who grew up in the hills of West Virginia and now makes his home on Long Island in New York. He has worked in the newspaper business for longer than he cares to admit, including twenty-three years at *Newsday* as a copy editor, page designer, and occasional feature writer. He has a bachelor's degree in editorial journalism from Marshall University in Huntington, West Virginia, and is married with two children, including a teenage son who is his sounding board and toughest critic. He is a Browns and Cubs fan, which, before the end of the curse in 2016, was about as much misery as a sports fan could stand. Naturally, he believes in the magic of Santa Claus and feels sorry for anyone who doesn't.